PLAGUED
THE MIRANDA CHRONICLES

WRITER
GARY CHUDLEIGH

ARTIST/COLOURS
TANYA ROBERTS

LETTERING
COLIN BELL

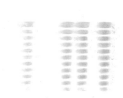

EDITOR
JACK LOTHIAN

PRODUCTION & DESIGN
SHA NAZIR
GREG WATT

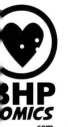

BHP COMICS
EXPANDING THE CULTURE OF COMIC BOOKS

Jack Lothian - Editor & Publisher
@Jack_Lothian

Sha Nazir - Art Director & Publisher
@sha_nazir

/BHPcomics @BHP_comics
/BHPcomics /BHPcomics

BHP COMICS .com

Plagued: The Miranda Chronicles | Volume 1. First printing. June 2016. Published in Glasgow by (BHP Comics) Black Hearted Press Ltd.

CHAPTER ONE

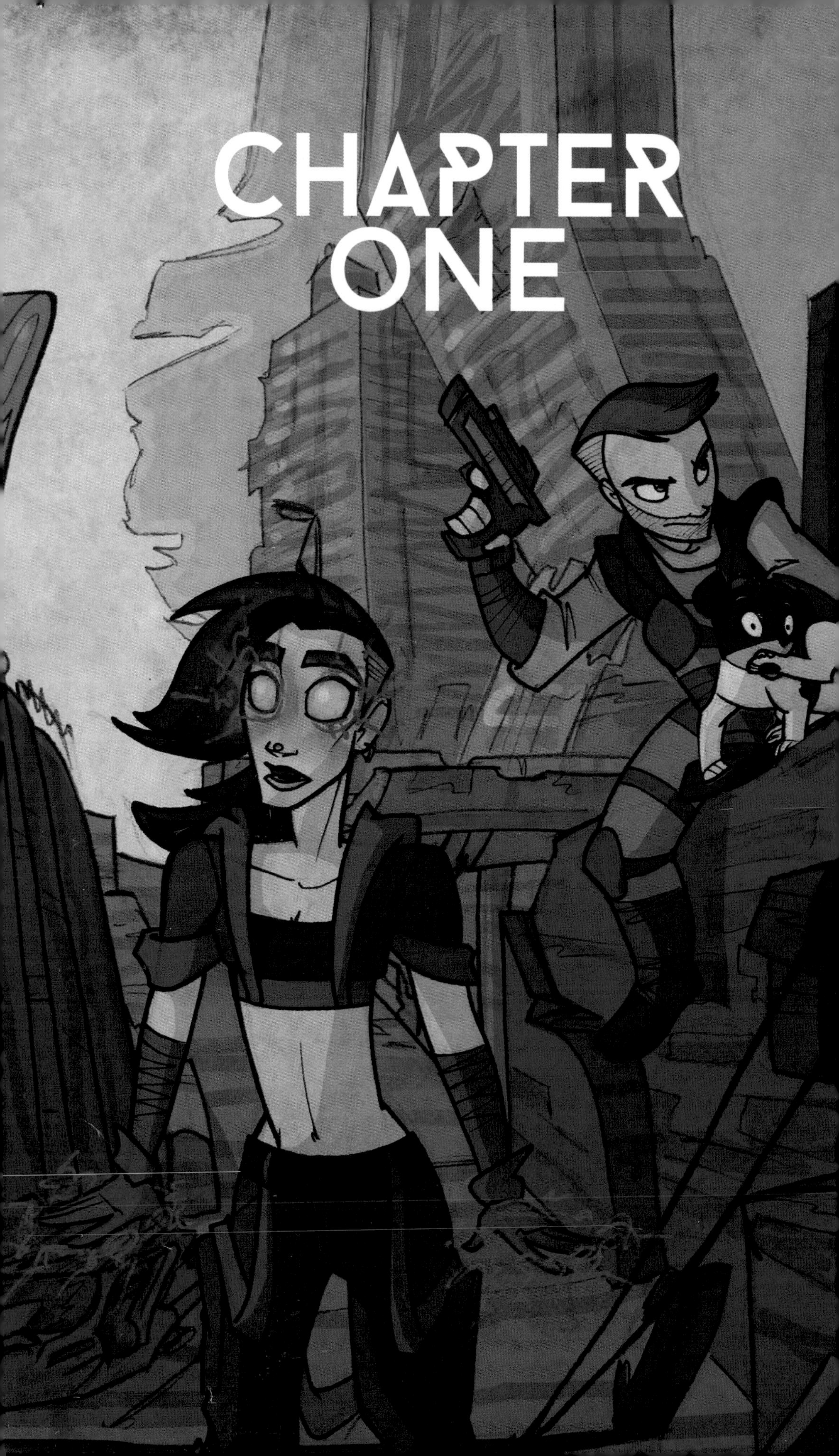

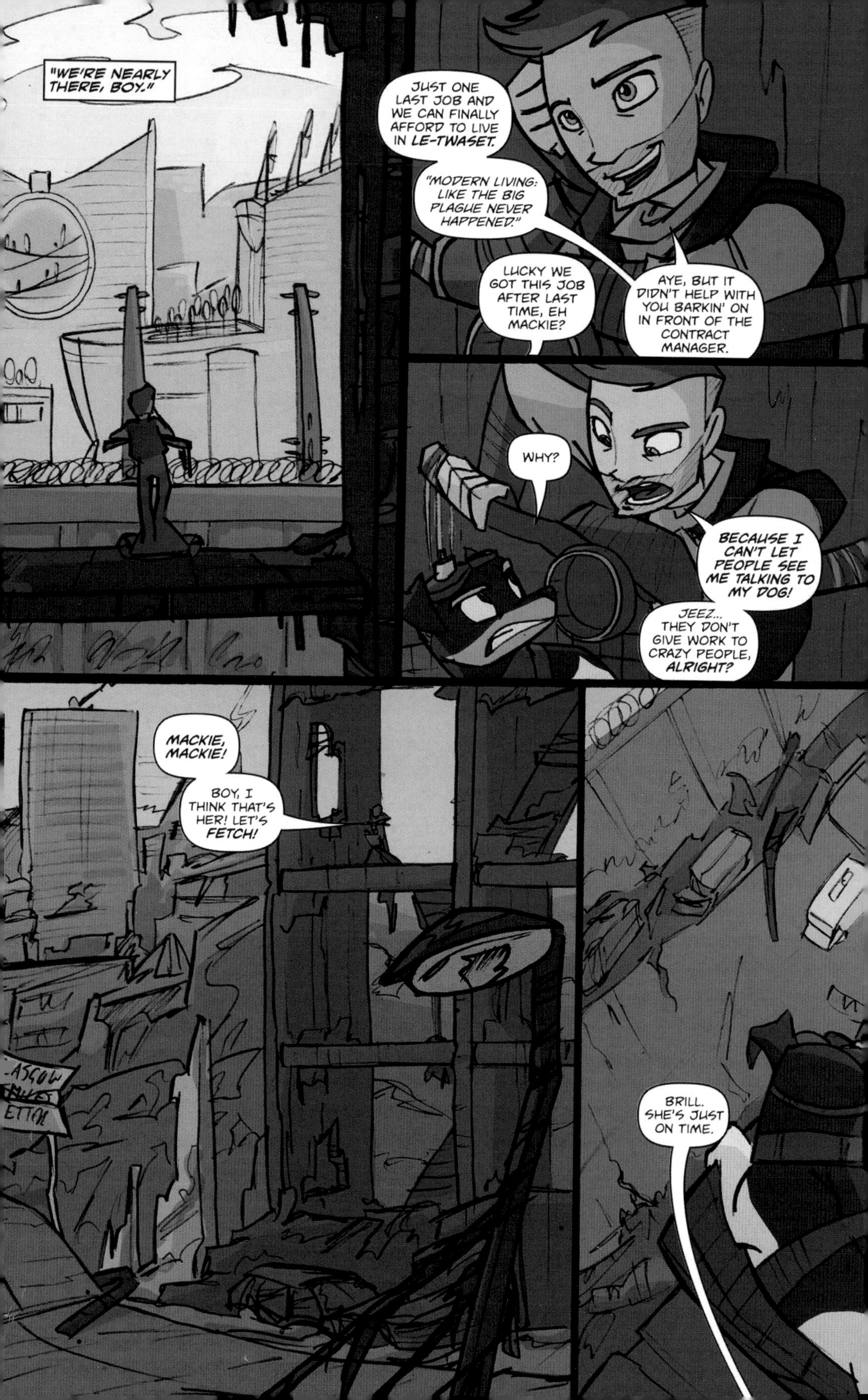
"WE'RE NEARLY THERE, BOY."
JUST ONE LAST JOB AND WE CAN FINALLY AFFORD TO LIVE IN LE-TWASET.
"MODERN LIVING: LIKE THE BIG PLAGUE NEVER HAPPENED."
LUCKY WE GOT THIS JOB AFTER LAST TIME, EH MACKIE?
AYE, BUT IT DIDN'T HELP WITH YOU BARKIN' ON IN FRONT OF THE CONTRACT MANAGER.
WHY?
BECAUSE I CAN'T LET PEOPLE SEE ME TALKING TO MY DOG!
JEEZ... THEY DON'T GIVE WORK TO CRAZY PEOPLE, ALRIGHT?
MACKIE, MACKIE!
BOY, I THINK THAT'S HER! LET'S FETCH!
BRILL. SHE'S JUST ON TIME.

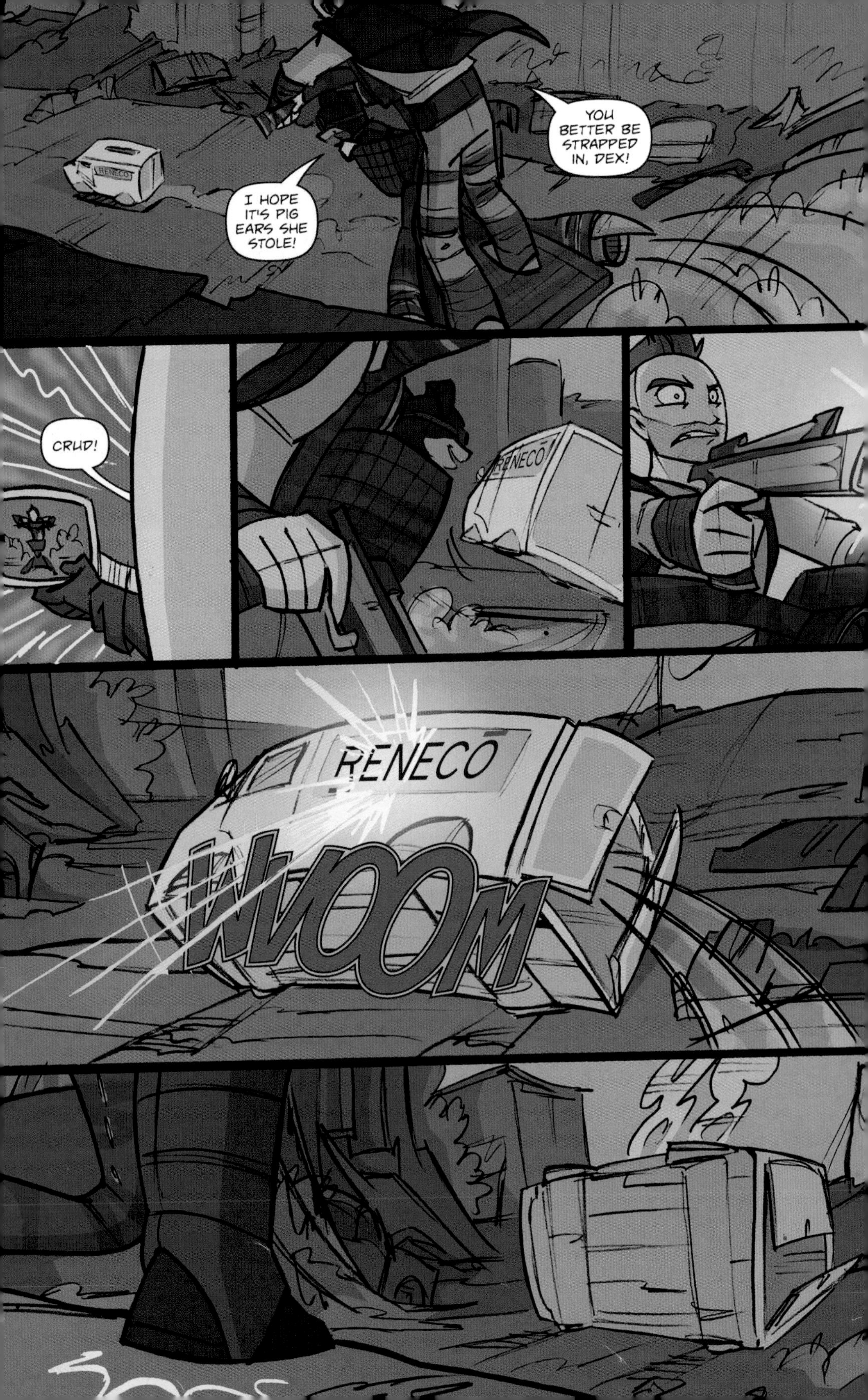
YOU BETTER BE STRAPPED IN, DEX!
I HOPE IT'S PIG EARS SHE STOLE!
RENECO
CRUD!
RENECO
RENECO
RENECO
WHOOM

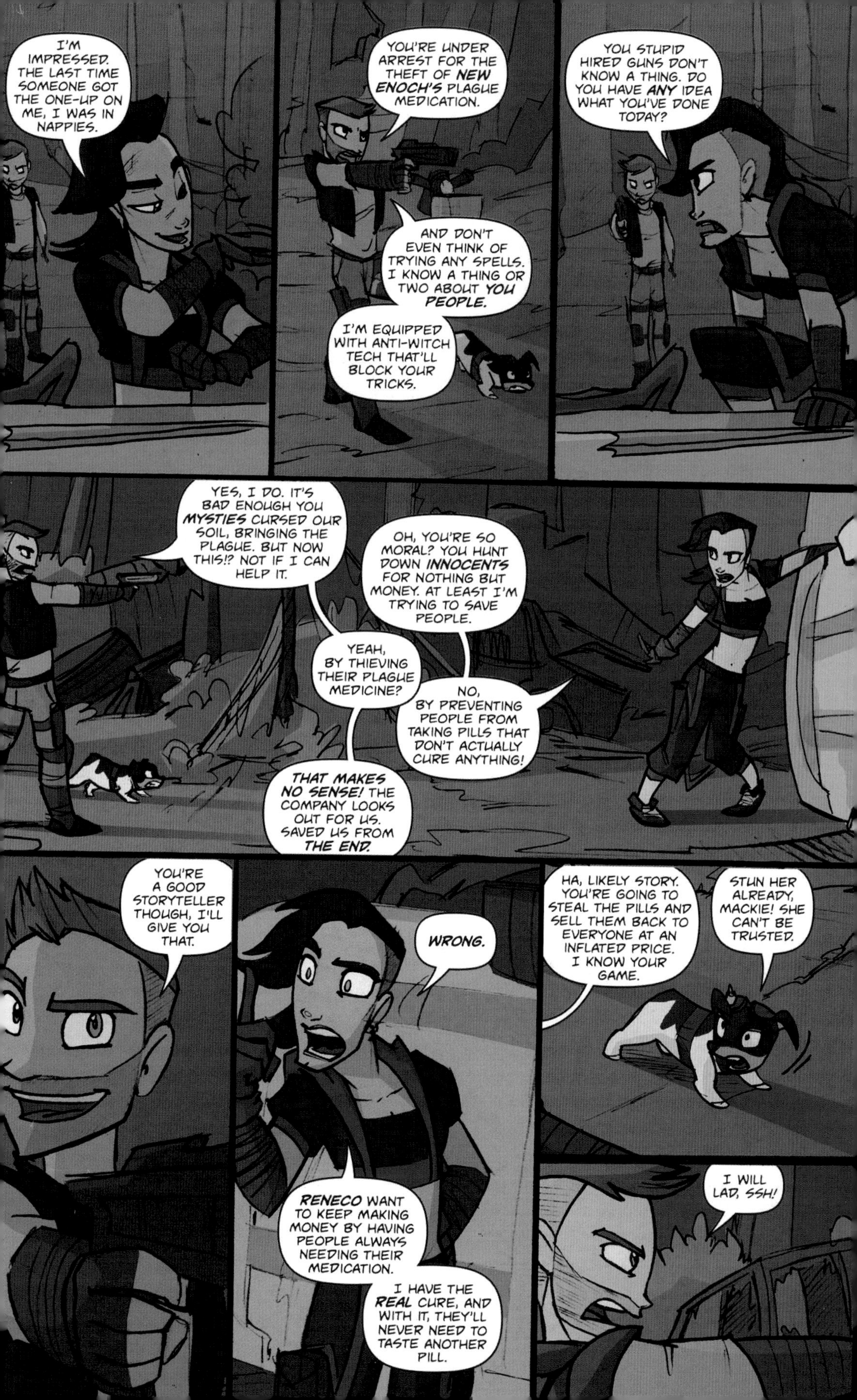
I'M IMPRESSED. THE LAST TIME SOMEONE GOT THE ONE-UP ON ME, I WAS IN NAPPIES.
YOU'RE UNDER ARREST FOR THE THEFT OF NEW ENOCH'S PLAGUE MEDICATION.
AND DON'T EVEN THINK OF TRYING ANY SPELLS. I KNOW A THING OR TWO ABOUT YOU PEOPLE.
I'M EQUIPPED WITH ANTI-WITCH TECH THAT'LL BLOCK YOUR TRICKS.
YOU STUPID HIRED GUNS DON'T KNOW A THING. DO YOU HAVE ANY IDEA WHAT YOU'VE DONE TODAY?
YES, I DO. IT'S BAD ENOUGH YOU MYSTIES CURSED OUR SOIL, BRINGING THE PLAGUE. BUT NOW THIS!? NOT IF I CAN HELP IT.
OH, YOU'RE SO MORAL? YOU HUNT DOWN INNOCENTS FOR NOTHING BUT MONEY. AT LEAST I'M TRYING TO SAVE PEOPLE.
YEAH, BY THIEVING THEIR PLAGUE MEDICINE?
NO, BY PREVENTING PEOPLE FROM TAKING PILLS THAT DON'T ACTUALLY CURE ANYTHING!
THAT MAKES NO SENSE! THE COMPANY LOOKS OUT FOR US. SAVED US FROM THE END.
YOU'RE A GOOD STORYTELLER THOUGH, I'LL GIVE YOU THAT.
WRONG.
RENECO WANT TO KEEP MAKING MONEY BY HAVING PEOPLE ALWAYS NEEDING THEIR MEDICATION.
I HAVE THE REAL CURE, AND WITH IT, THEY'LL NEVER NEED TO TASTE ANOTHER PILL.
HA, LIKELY STORY. YOU'RE GOING TO STEAL THE PILLS AND SELL THEM BACK TO EVERYONE AT AN INFLATED PRICE. I KNOW YOUR GAME.
STUN HER ALREADY, MACKIE! SHE CAN'T BE TRUSTED.
I WILL LAD, SSH!

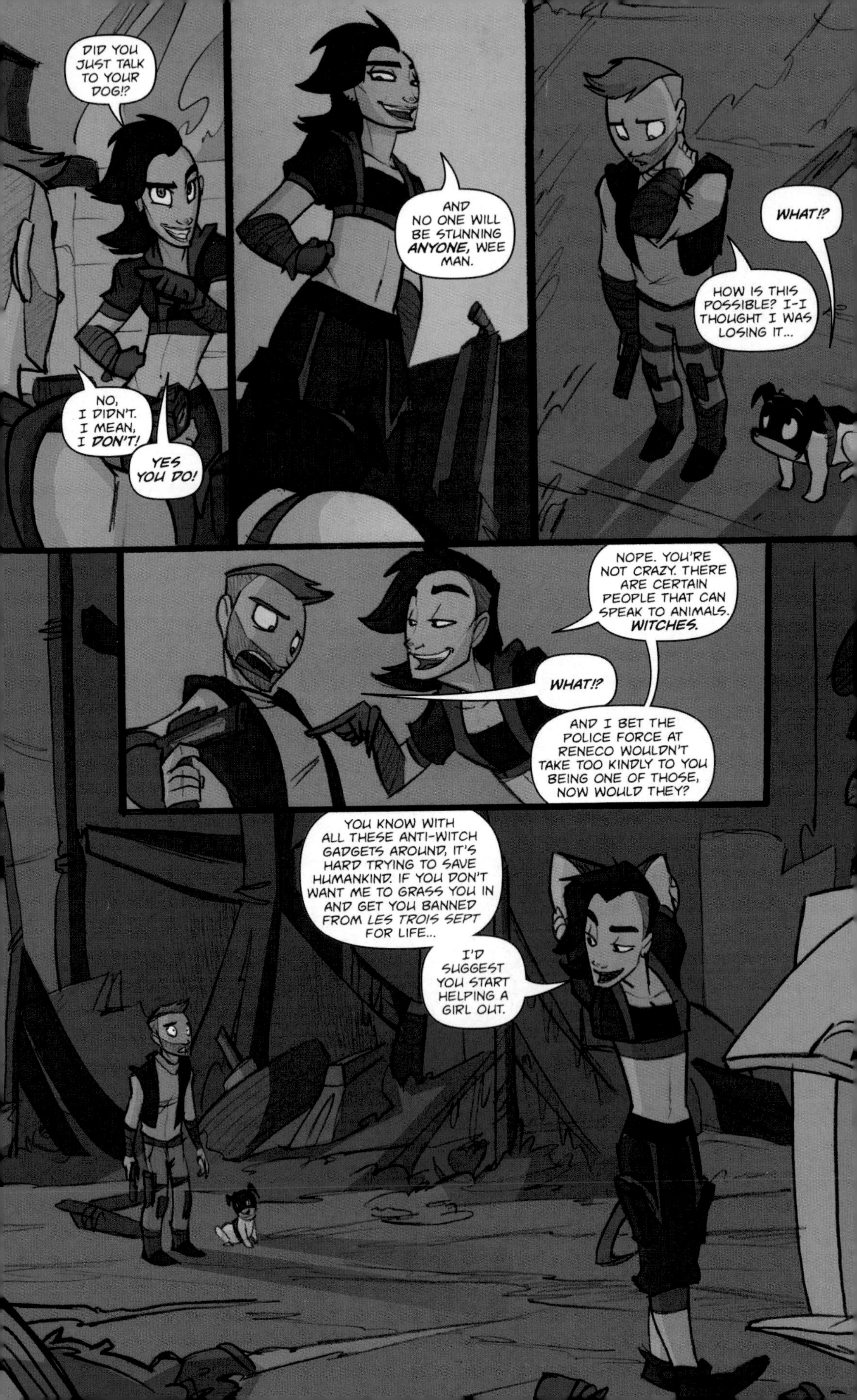

DID YOU JUST TALK TO YOUR DOG!?
NO, I DIDN'T. I MEAN, I DON'T!
YES YOU DO!
AND NO ONE WILL BE STUNNING ANYONE, WEE MAN.
HOW IS THIS POSSIBLE? I-I THOUGHT I WAS LOSING IT...
WHAT!?
NOPE. YOU'RE NOT CRAZY. THERE ARE CERTAIN PEOPLE THAT CAN SPEAK TO ANIMALS. WITCHES.
WHAT!?
AND I BET THE POLICE FORCE AT RENECO WOULDN'T TAKE TOO KINDLY TO YOU BEING ONE OF THOSE, NOW WOULD THEY?
YOU KNOW WITH ALL THESE ANTI-WITCH GADGETS AROUND, IT'S HARD TRYING TO SAVE HUMANKIND. IF YOU DON'T WANT ME TO GRASS YOU IN AND GET YOU BANNED FROM LES TROIS SEPT FOR LIFE...
I'D SUGGEST YOU START HELPING A GIRL OUT.

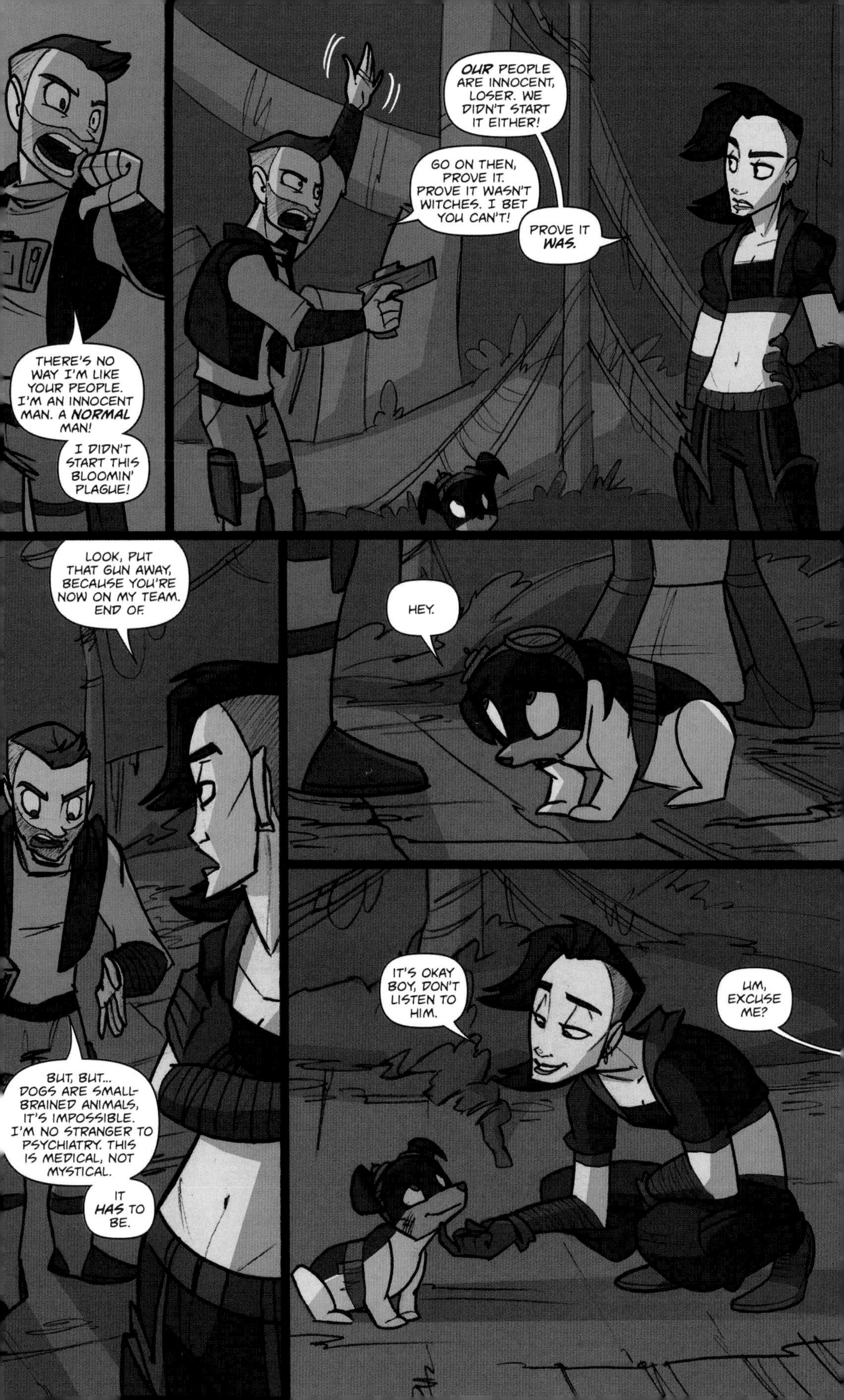

THERE'S NO WAY I'M LIKE YOUR PEOPLE. I'M AN INNOCENT MAN. A **NORMAL** MAN!
I DIDN'T START THIS BLOOMIN' PLAGUE!
OUR PEOPLE ARE INNOCENT, LOSER. WE DIDN'T START IT EITHER!
GO ON THEN, PROVE IT. PROVE IT WASN'T WITCHES. I BET YOU CAN'T!
PROVE IT **WAS.**
LOOK, PUT THAT GUN AWAY, BECAUSE YOU'RE NOW ON MY TEAM. END OF.
BUT, BUT... DOGS ARE SMALL-BRAINED ANIMALS, IT'S IMPOSSIBLE. I'M NO STRANGER TO PSYCHIATRY. THIS IS MEDICAL, NOT MYSTICAL.
IT **HAS** TO BE.
HEY.
IT'S OKAY BOY, DON'T LISTEN TO HIM.
UM, EXCUSE ME?

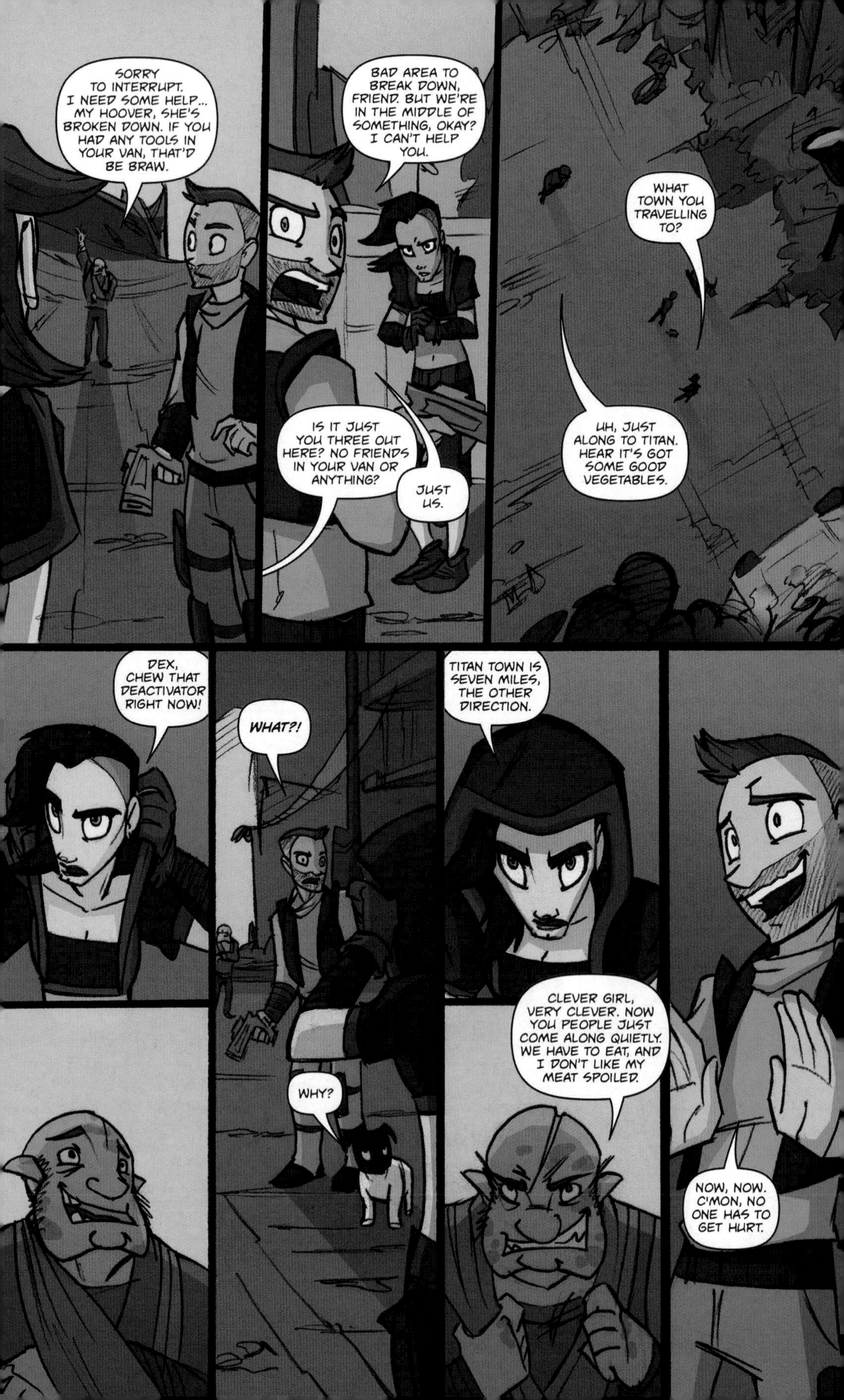
SORRY TO INTERRUPT. I NEED SOME HELP... MY HOOVER, SHE'S BROKEN DOWN. IF YOU HAD ANY TOOLS IN YOUR VAN, THAT'D BE BRAW.
BAD AREA TO BREAK DOWN, FRIEND. BUT WE'RE IN THE MIDDLE OF SOMETHING, OKAY? I CAN'T HELP YOU.
IS IT JUST YOU THREE OUT HERE? NO FRIENDS IN YOUR VAN OR ANYTHING?
JUST US.
WHAT TOWN YOU TRAVELLING TO?
UH, JUST ALONG TO TITAN. HEAR IT'S GOT SOME GOOD VEGETABLES.
DEX, CHEW THAT DEACTIVATOR RIGHT NOW!
WHAT?!
WHY?
TITAN TOWN IS SEVEN MILES, THE OTHER DIRECTION.
CLEVER GIRL, VERY CLEVER. NOW YOU PEOPLE JUST COME ALONG QUIETLY. WE HAVE TO EAT, AND I DON'T LIKE MY MEAT SPOILED.
NOW, NOW. C'MON, NO ONE HAS TO GET HURT.

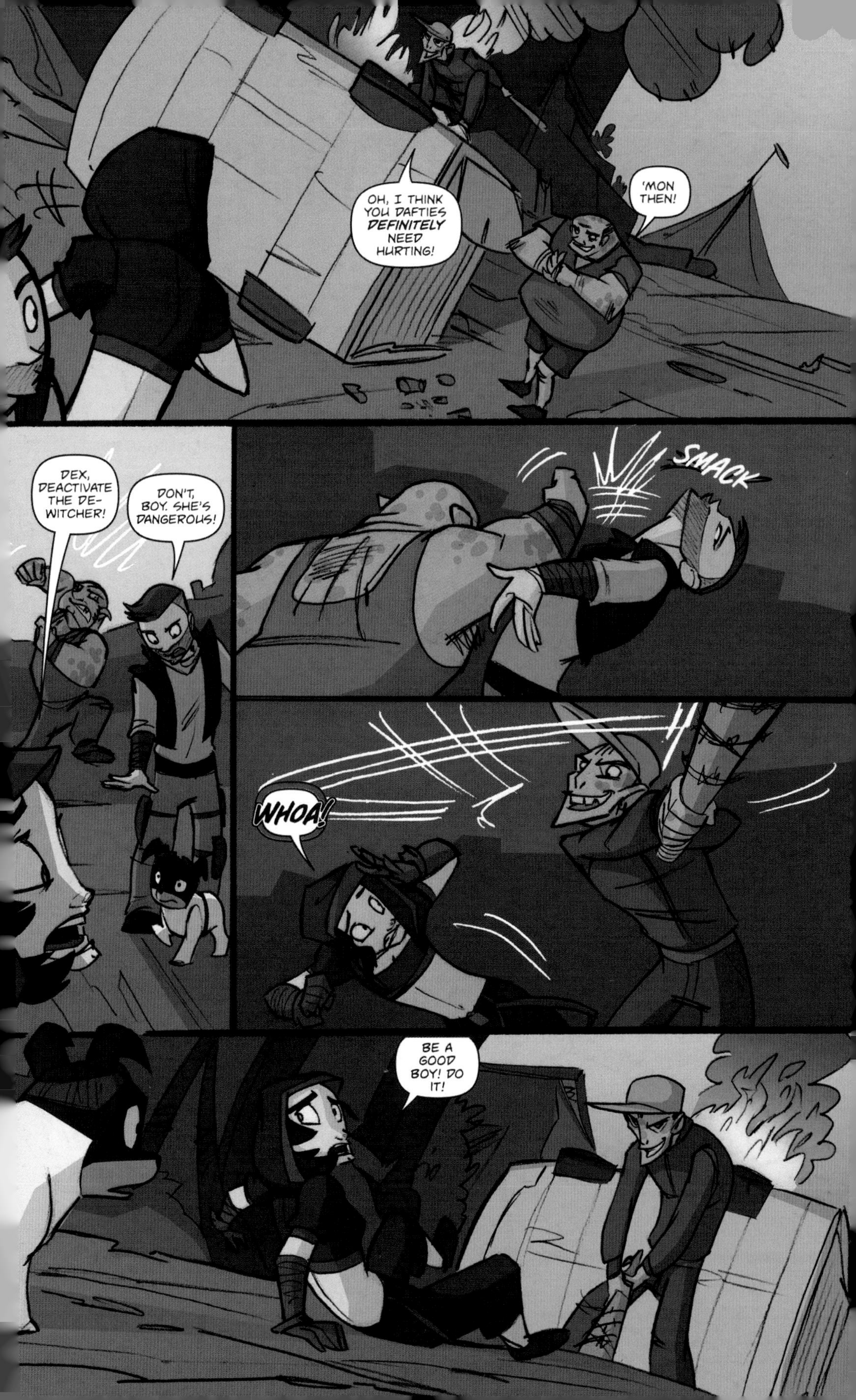
OH, I THINK YOU DAFTIES DEFINITELY NEED HURTING!
'MON THEN!
DEX, DEACTIVATE THE DE-WITCHER!
DON'T, BOY. SHE'S DANGEROUS!
SMACK
WHOA!
BE A GOOD BOY! DO IT!

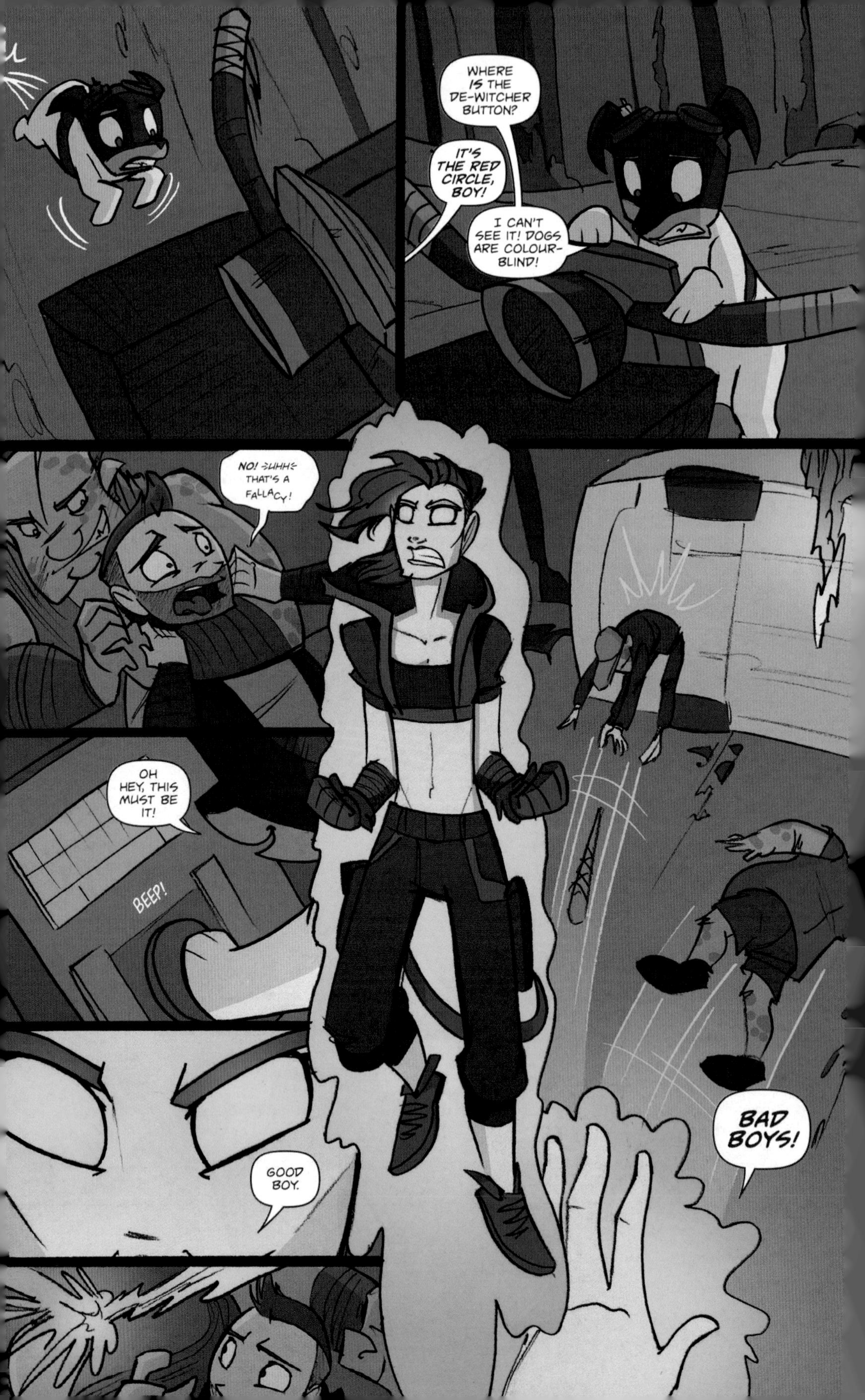
WHERE *IS* THE DE-WITCHER BUTTON?
IT'S THE RED CIRCLE, BOY!
I CAN'T SEE IT! DOGS ARE COLOUR-BLIND!
NO! ƸUHHƸ THAT'S A FALLACY!
OH HEY, THIS MUST BE IT!
BEEP!
GOOD BOY.
BAD BOYS!

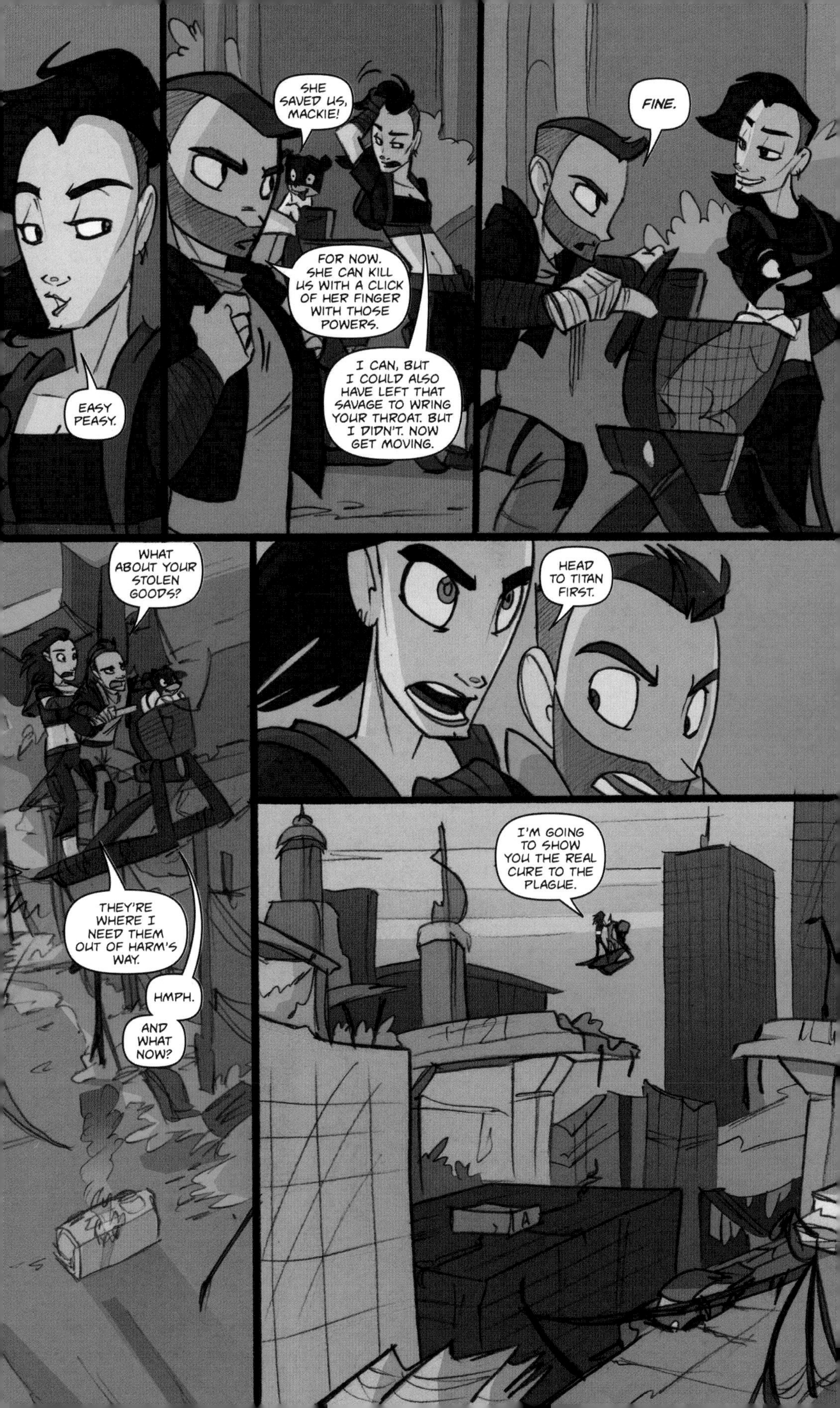
EASY PEASY.
SHE SAVED US, MACKIE!
FOR NOW. SHE CAN KILL US WITH A CLICK OF HER FINGER WITH THOSE POWERS.
I CAN, BUT I COULD ALSO HAVE LEFT THAT SAVAGE TO WRING YOUR THROAT. BUT I DIDN'T. NOW GET MOVING.
FINE.
WHAT ABOUT YOUR STOLEN GOODS?
THEY'RE WHERE I NEED THEM OUT OF HARM'S WAY.
HMPH.
AND WHAT NOW?
HEAD TO TITAN FIRST.
I'M GOING TO SHOW YOU THE REAL CURE TO THE PLAGUE.

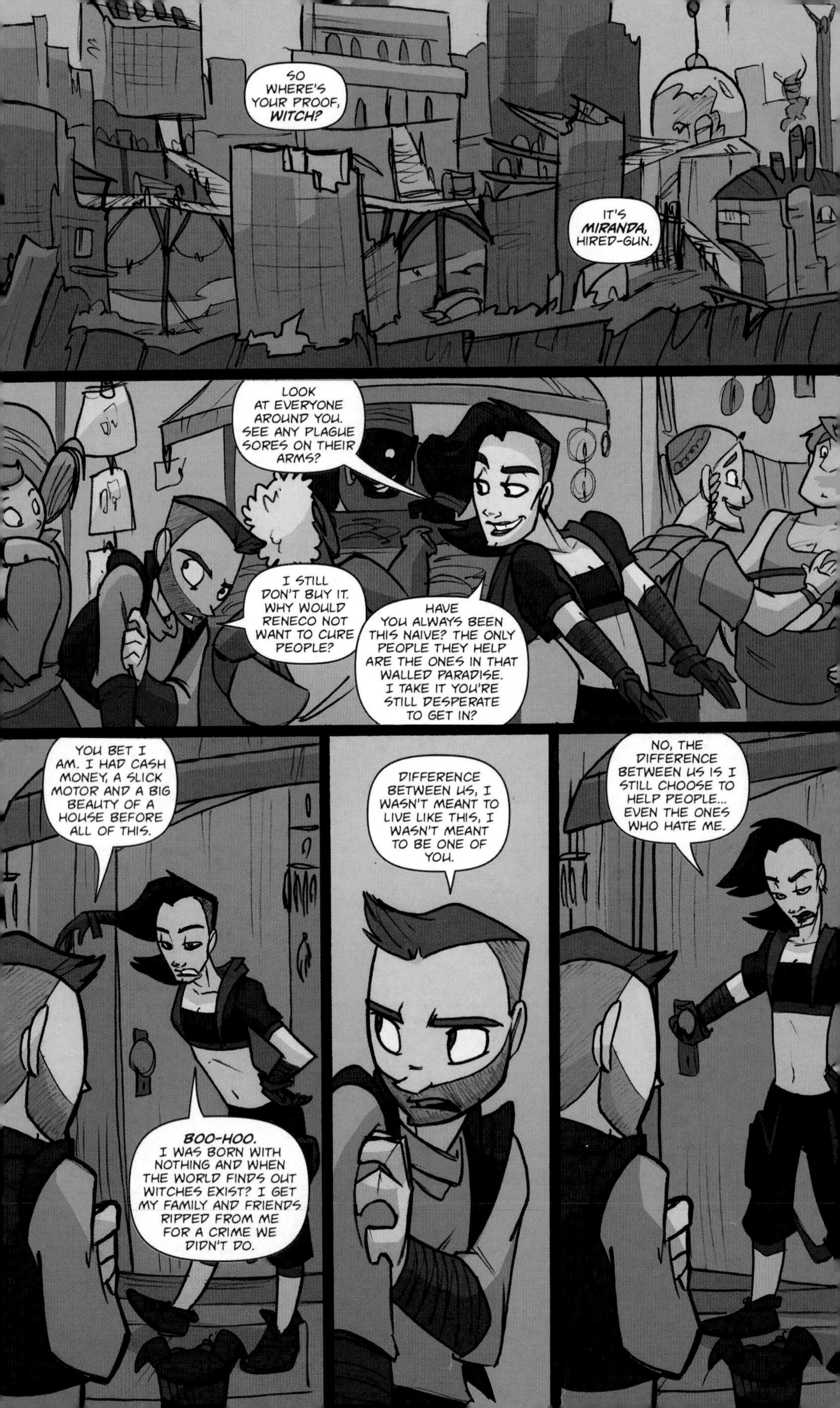

SO WHERE'S YOUR PROOF, WITCH?
IT'S MIRANDA, HIRED-GUN.
LOOK AT EVERYONE AROUND YOU. SEE ANY PLAGUE SORES ON THEIR ARMS?
I STILL DON'T BUY IT. WHY WOULD RENECO NOT WANT TO CURE PEOPLE?
HAVE YOU ALWAYS BEEN THIS NAIVE? THE ONLY PEOPLE THEY HELP ARE THE ONES IN THAT WALLED PARADISE. I TAKE IT YOU'RE STILL DESPERATE TO GET IN?
YOU BET I AM. I HAD CASH MONEY, A SLICK MOTOR AND A BIG BEAUTY OF A HOUSE BEFORE ALL OF THIS.
BOO-HOO. I WAS BORN WITH NOTHING AND WHEN THE WORLD FINDS OUT WITCHES EXIST? I GET MY FAMILY AND FRIENDS RIPPED FROM ME FOR A CRIME WE DIDN'T DO.
DIFFERENCE BETWEEN US, I WASN'T MEANT TO LIVE LIKE THIS, I WASN'T MEANT TO BE ONE OF YOU.
NO, THE DIFFERENCE BETWEEN US IS I STILL CHOOSE TO HELP PEOPLE... EVEN THE ONES WHO HATE ME.

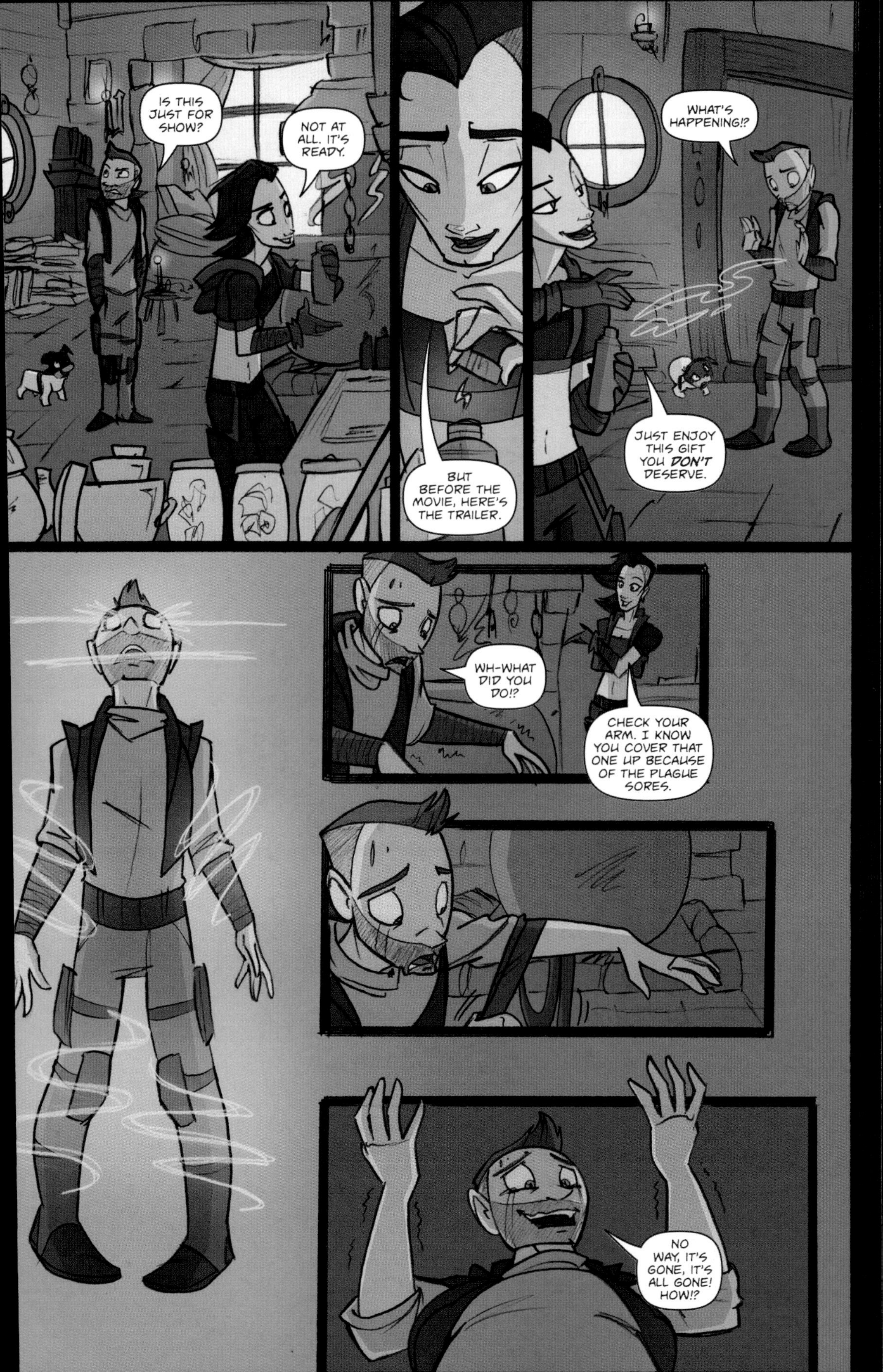

IS THIS JUST FOR SHOW?
NOT AT ALL. IT'S READY.
BUT BEFORE THE MOVIE, HERE'S THE TRAILER.
WHAT'S HAPPENING!?
JUST ENJOY THIS GIFT YOU **DON'T** DESERVE.
WH-WHAT DID YOU DO!?
CHECK YOUR ARM. I KNOW YOU COVER THAT ONE UP BECAUSE OF THE PLAGUE SORES.
NO WAY, IT'S GONE, IT'S ALL GONE! HOW!?

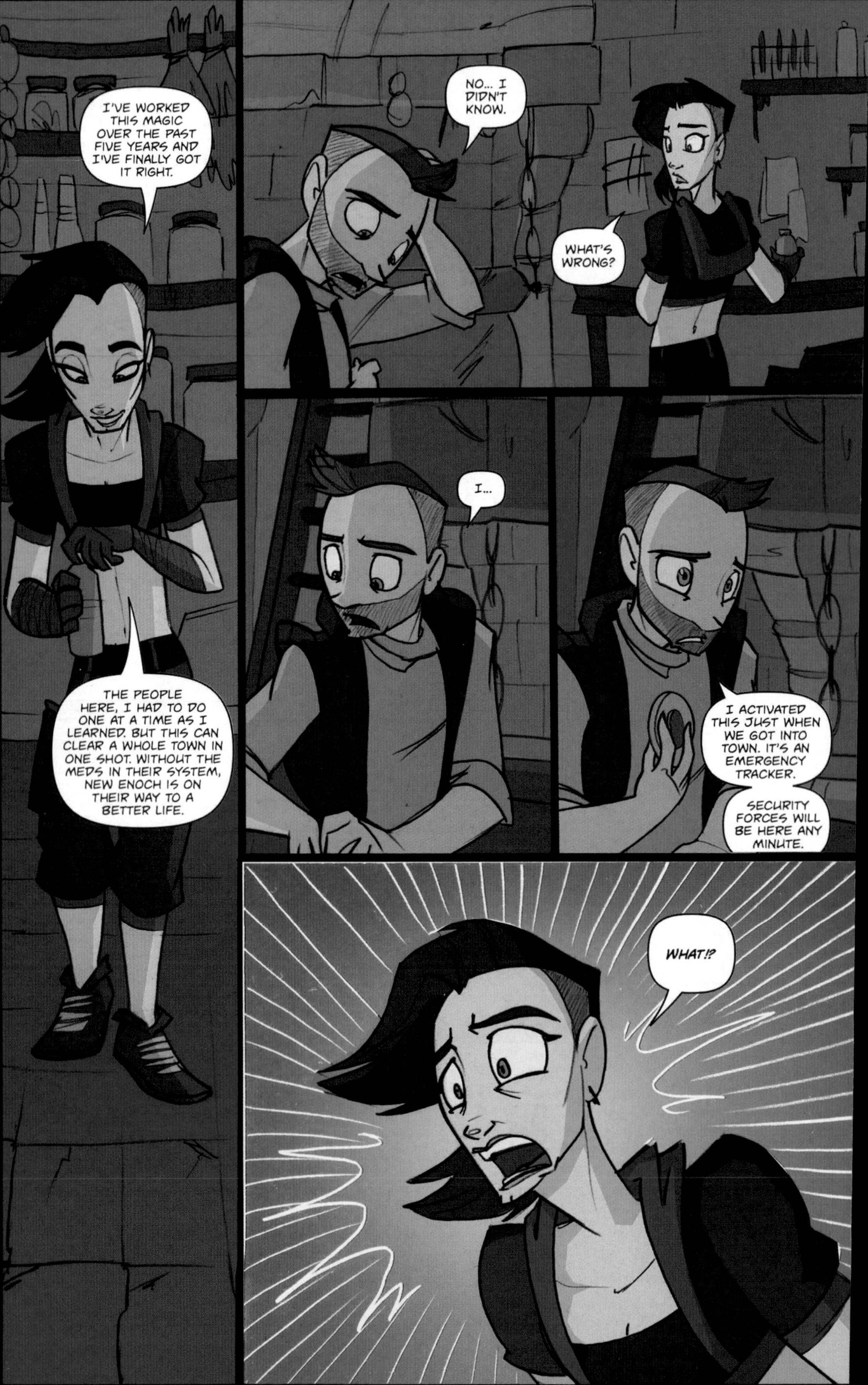
I'VE WORKED THIS MAGIC OVER THE PAST FIVE YEARS AND I'VE FINALLY GOT IT RIGHT.
THE PEOPLE HERE, I HAD TO DO ONE AT A TIME AS I LEARNED. BUT THIS CAN CLEAR A WHOLE TOWN IN ONE SHOT. WITHOUT THE MEDS IN THEIR SYSTEM, NEW ENOCH IS ON THEIR WAY TO A BETTER LIFE.
NO... I DIDN'T KNOW.
WHAT'S WRONG?
I...
I ACTIVATED THIS JUST WHEN WE GOT INTO TOWN. IT'S AN EMERGENCY TRACKER.
SECURITY FORCES WILL BE HERE ANY MINUTE.
WHAT!?

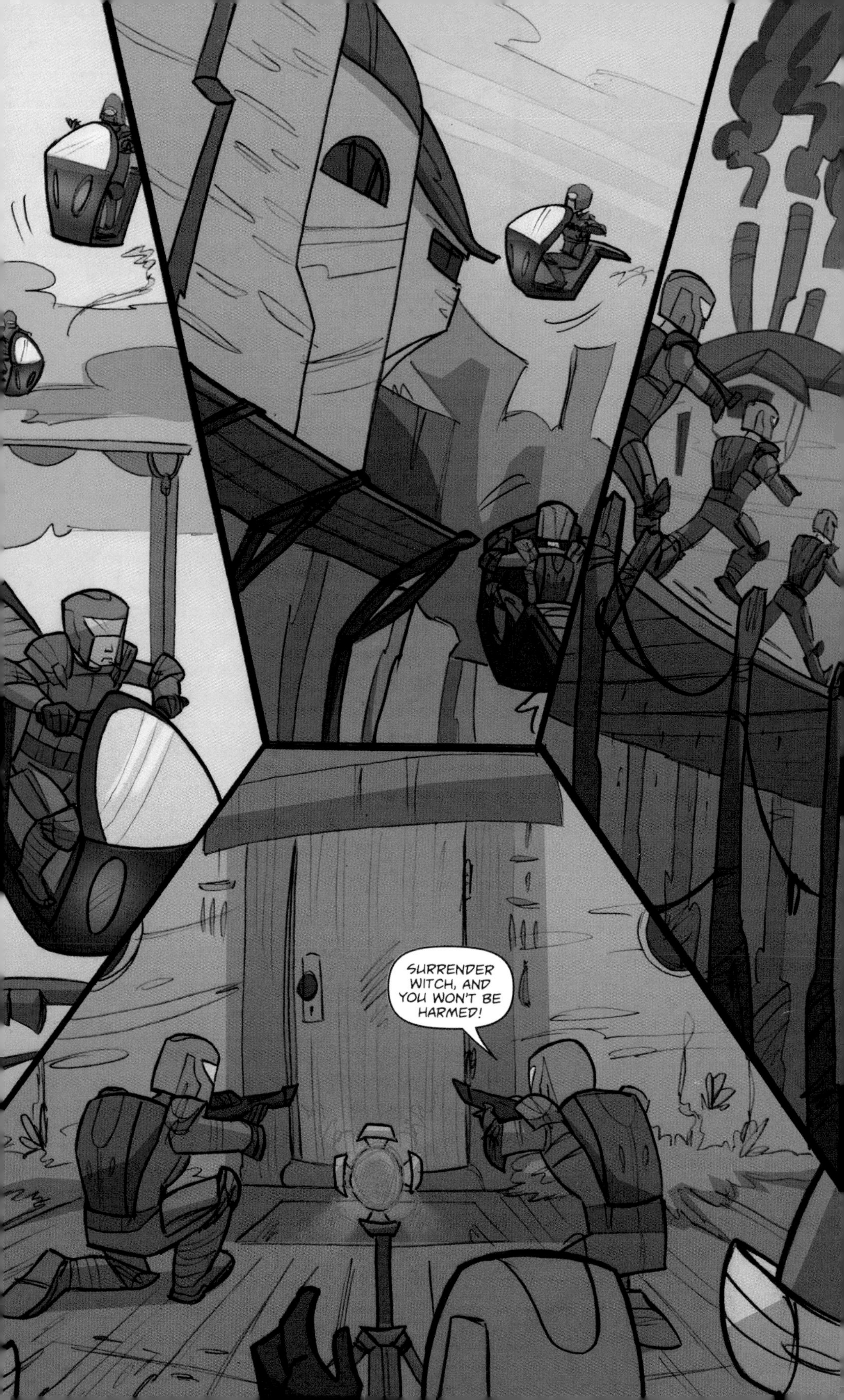
SURRENDER WITCH, AND YOU WON'T BE HARMED!

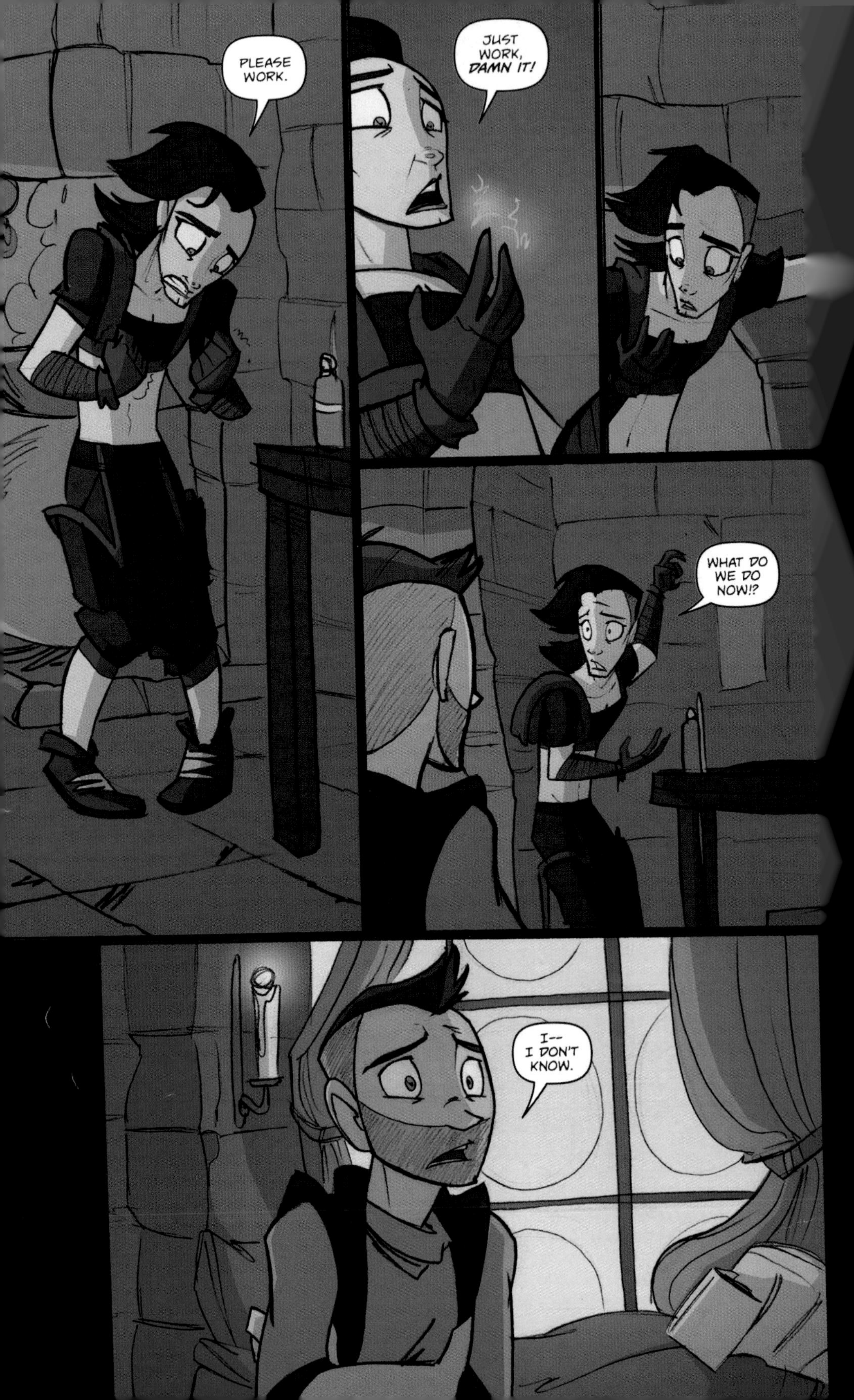
PLEASE WORK.
JUST WORK, *DAMN IT!*
WHAT DO WE DO NOW!?
I-- I DON'T KNOW.

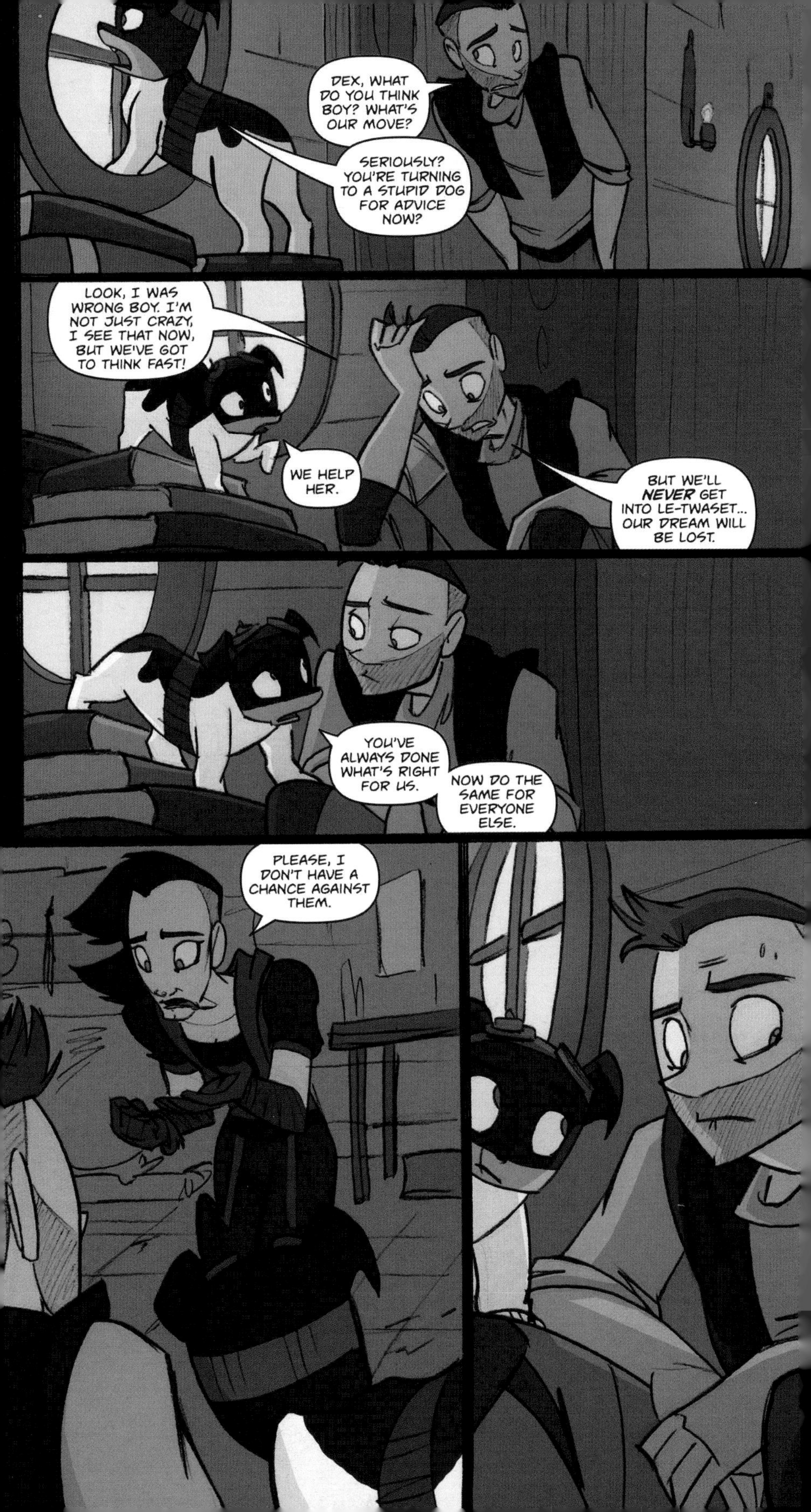
DEX, WHAT DO YOU THINK BOY? WHAT'S OUR MOVE?
SERIOUSLY? YOU'RE TURNING TO A STUPID DOG FOR ADVICE NOW?
LOOK, I WAS WRONG BOY. I'M NOT JUST CRAZY, I SEE THAT NOW, BUT WE'VE GOT TO THINK FAST!
WE HELP HER.
BUT WE'LL NEVER GET INTO LE-TWASET... OUR DREAM WILL BE LOST.
YOU'VE ALWAYS DONE WHAT'S RIGHT FOR US.
NOW DO THE SAME FOR EVERYONE ELSE.
PLEASE, I DON'T HAVE A CHANCE AGAINST THEM.

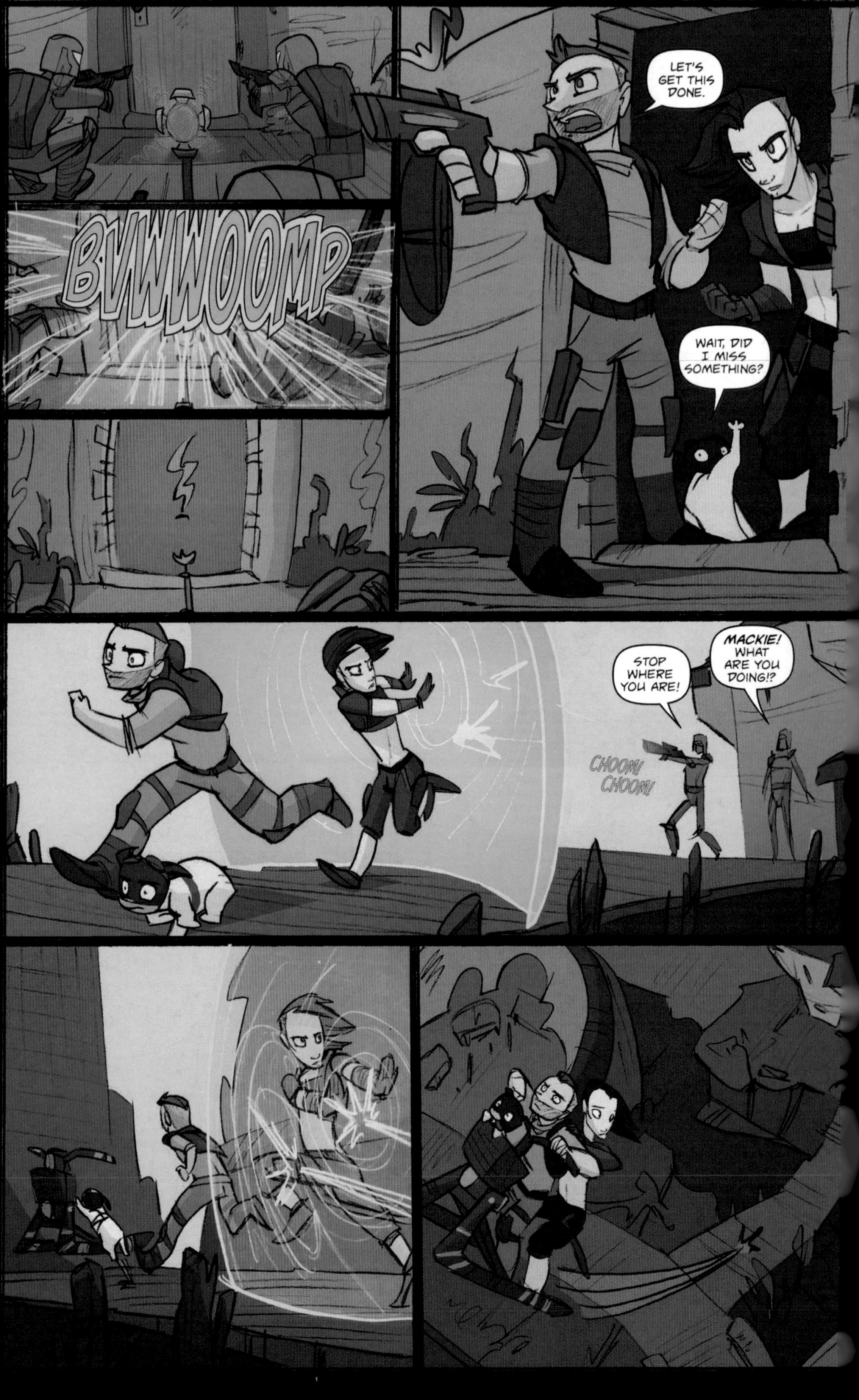
BVWWOOMP
LET'S GET THIS DONE.
WAIT, DID I MISS SOMETHING?
CHOOM! CHOOM!
STOP WHERE YOU ARE!
MACKIE! WHAT ARE YOU DOING!?

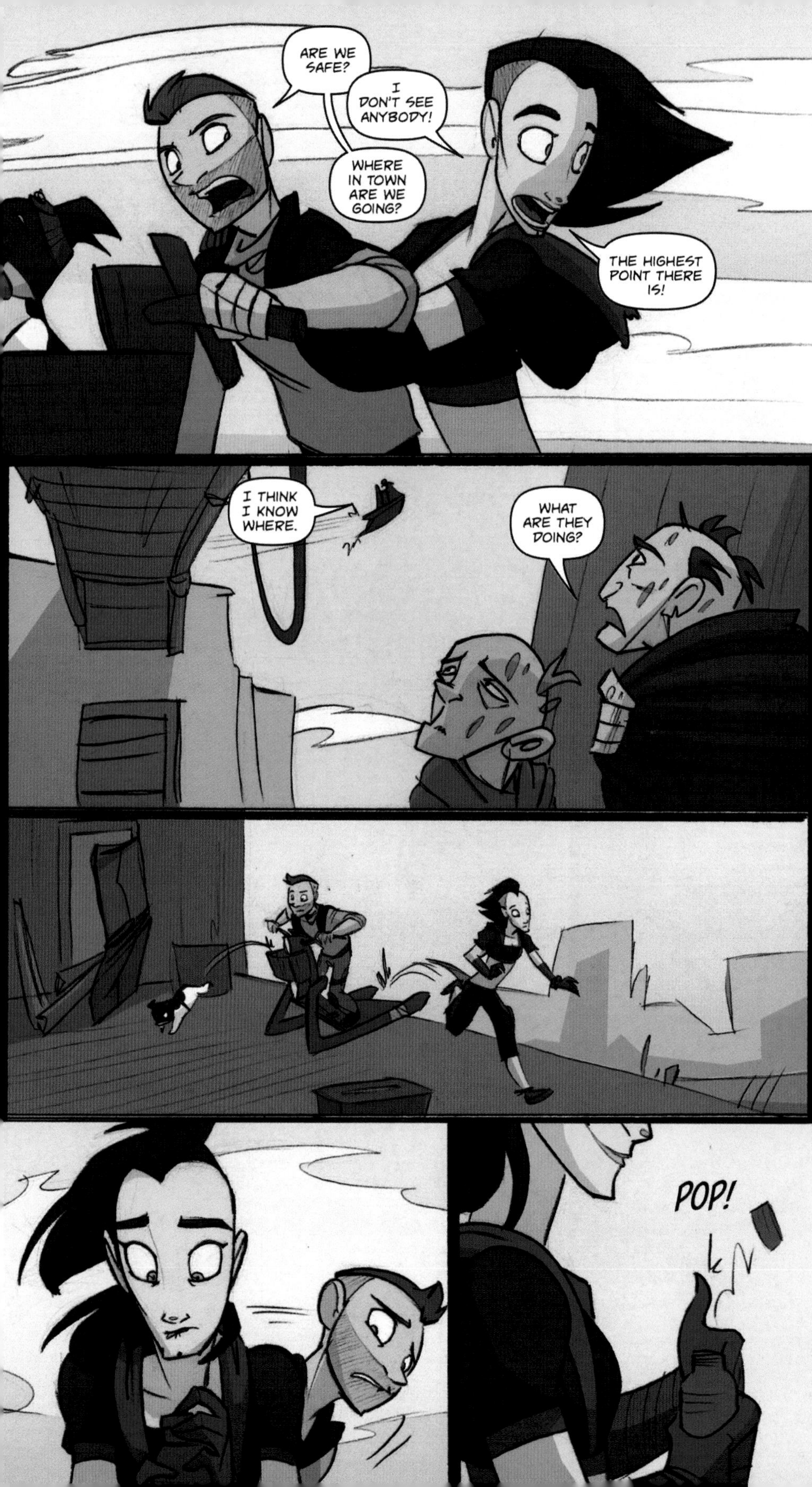
ARE WE SAFE?
I DON'T SEE ANYBODY!
WHERE IN TOWN ARE WE GOING?
THE HIGHEST POINT THERE IS!
I THINK I KNOW WHERE.
WHAT ARE THEY DOING?
POP!

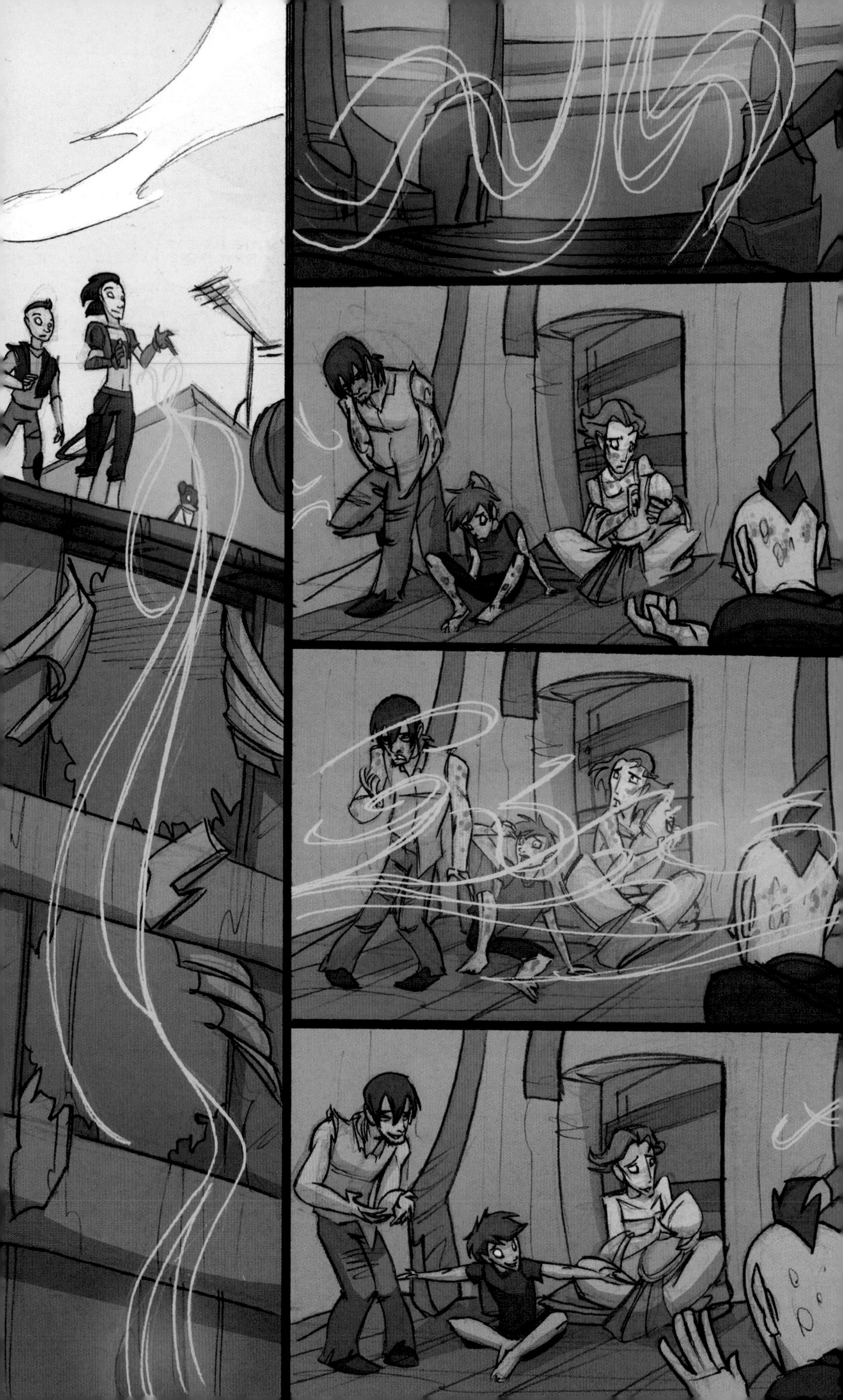

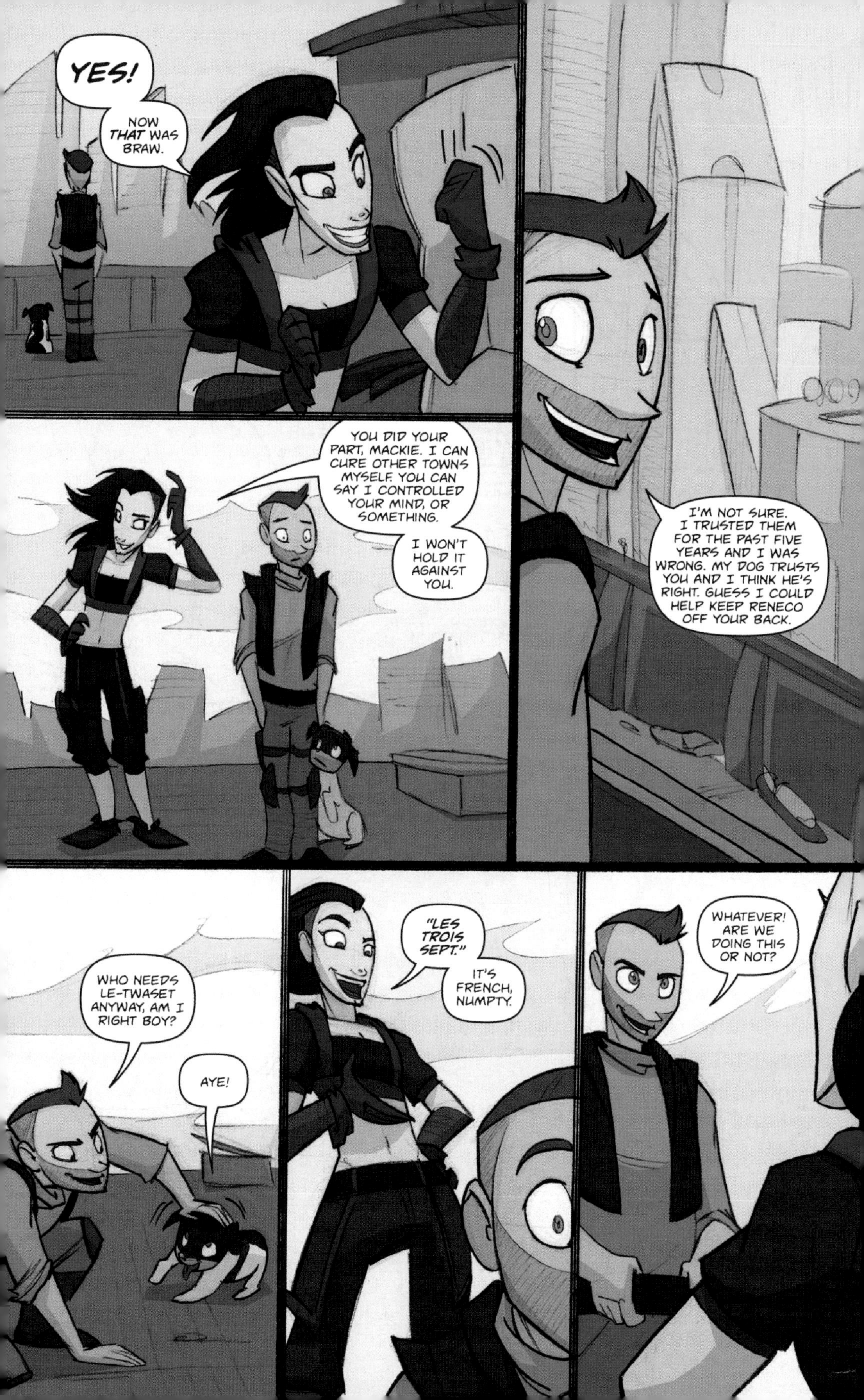
YES!
NOW *THAT* WAS BRAW.
YOU DID YOUR PART, MACKIE. I CAN CURE OTHER TOWNS MYSELF. YOU CAN SAY I CONTROLLED YOUR MIND, OR SOMETHING.
I WON'T HOLD IT AGAINST YOU.
I'M NOT SURE. I TRUSTED THEM FOR THE PAST FIVE YEARS AND I WAS WRONG. MY DOG TRUSTS YOU AND I THINK HE'S RIGHT. GUESS I COULD HELP KEEP RENECO OFF YOUR BACK.
WHO NEEDS LE-TWASET ANYWAY, AM I RIGHT BOY?
AYE!
"LES TROIS SEPT."
IT'S FRENCH, NUMPTY.
WHATEVER! ARE WE DOING THIS OR NOT?

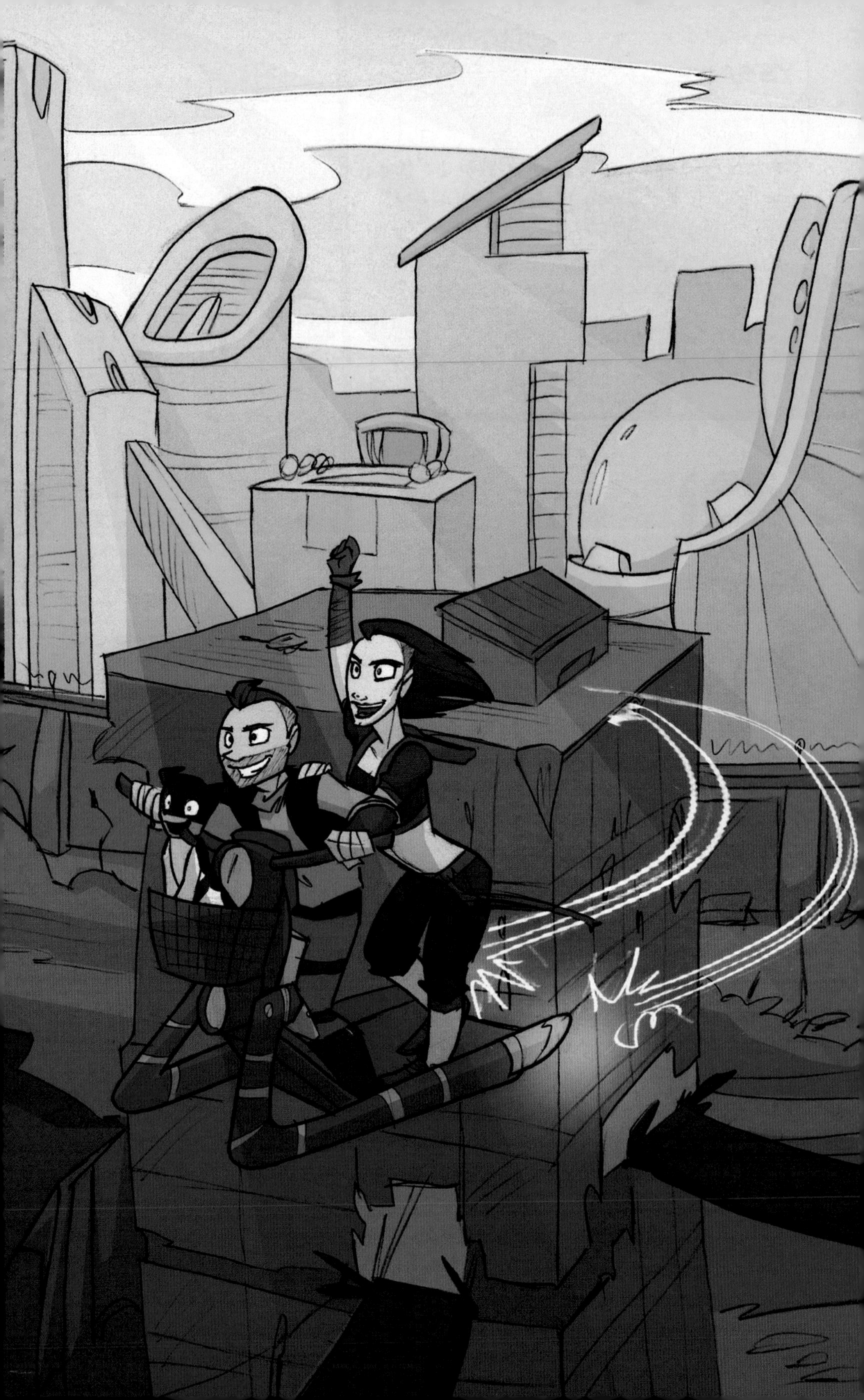

CHAPTER TWO

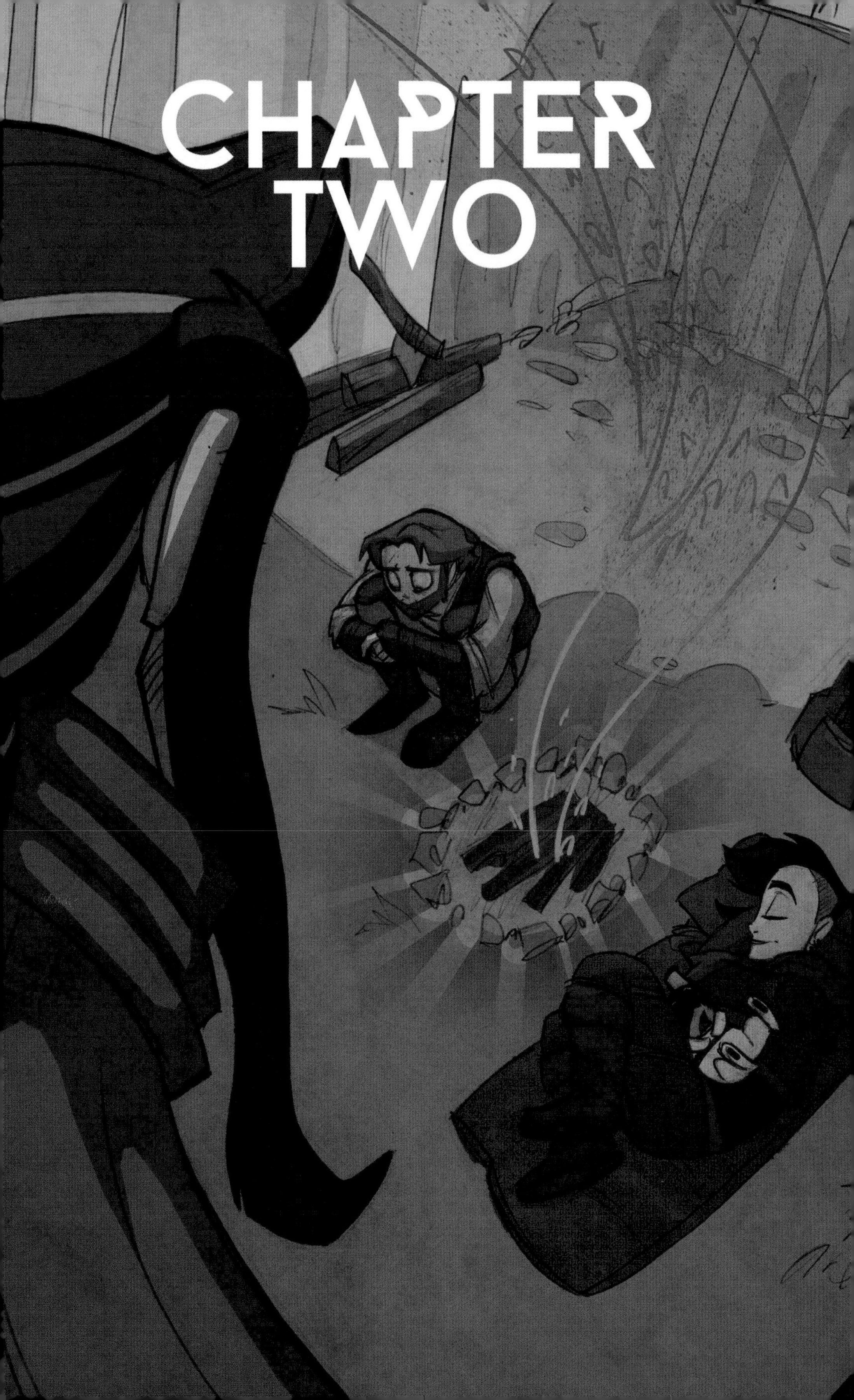

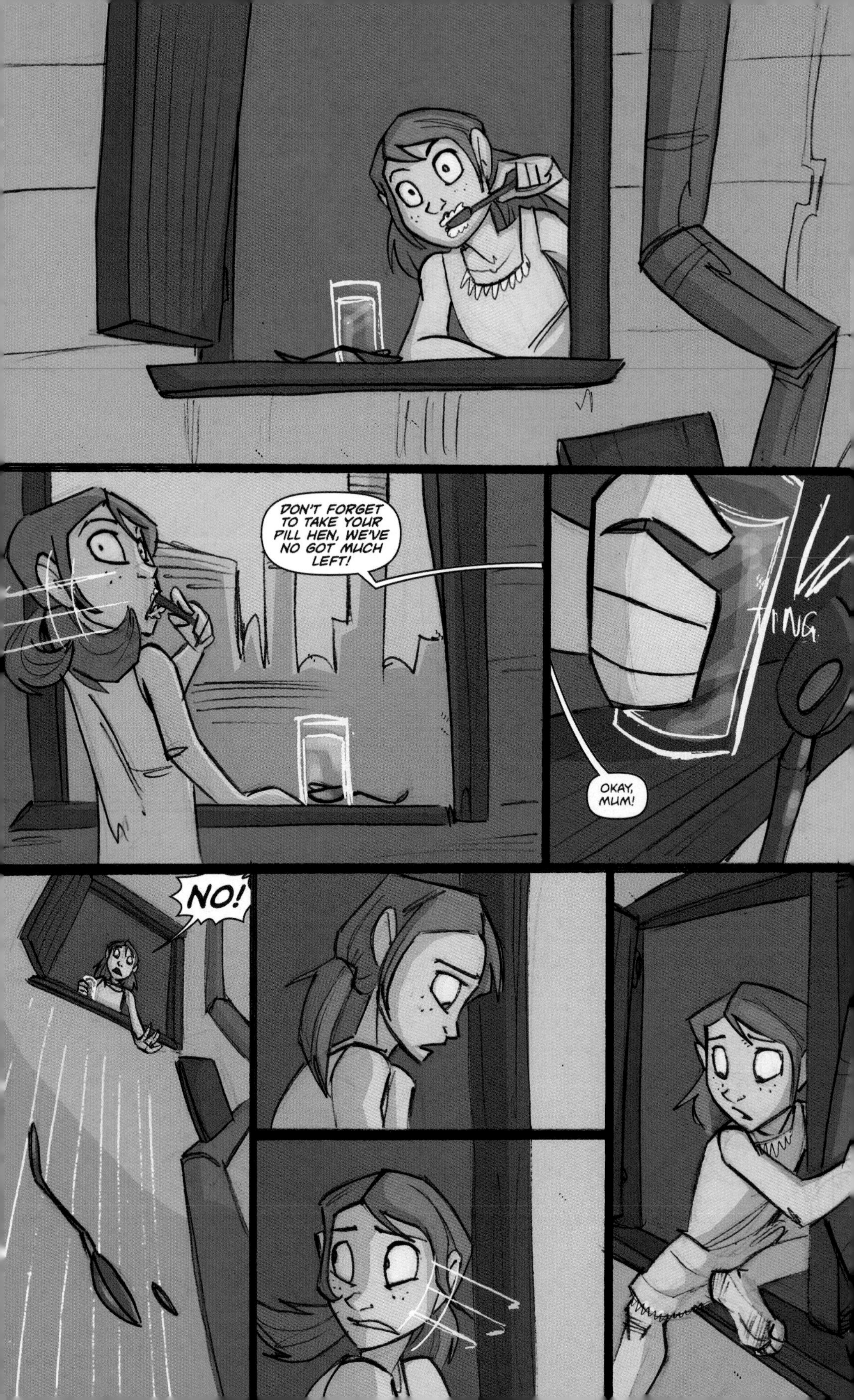
DON'T FORGET TO TAKE YOUR PILL HEN, WE'VE NO GOT MUCH LEFT!
TING
OKAY, MUM!
NO!

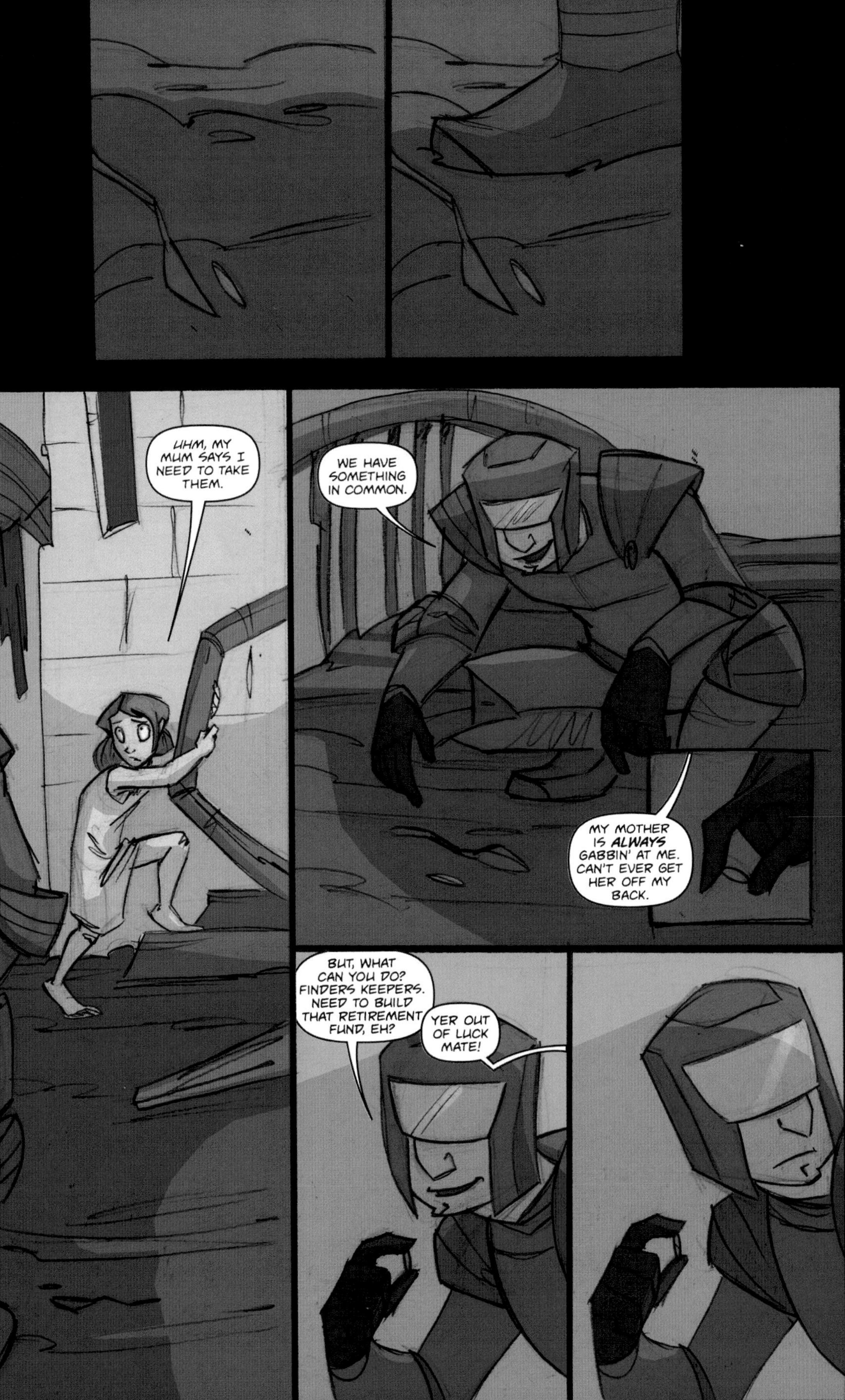
UHM, MY MUM SAYS I NEED TO TAKE THEM.
WE HAVE SOMETHING IN COMMON.
MY MOTHER IS ALWAYS GABBIN' AT ME. CAN'T EVER GET HER OFF MY BACK.
BUT, WHAT CAN YOU DO? FINDERS KEEPERS. NEED TO BUILD THAT RETIREMENT FUND, EH?
YER OUT OF LUCK MATE!

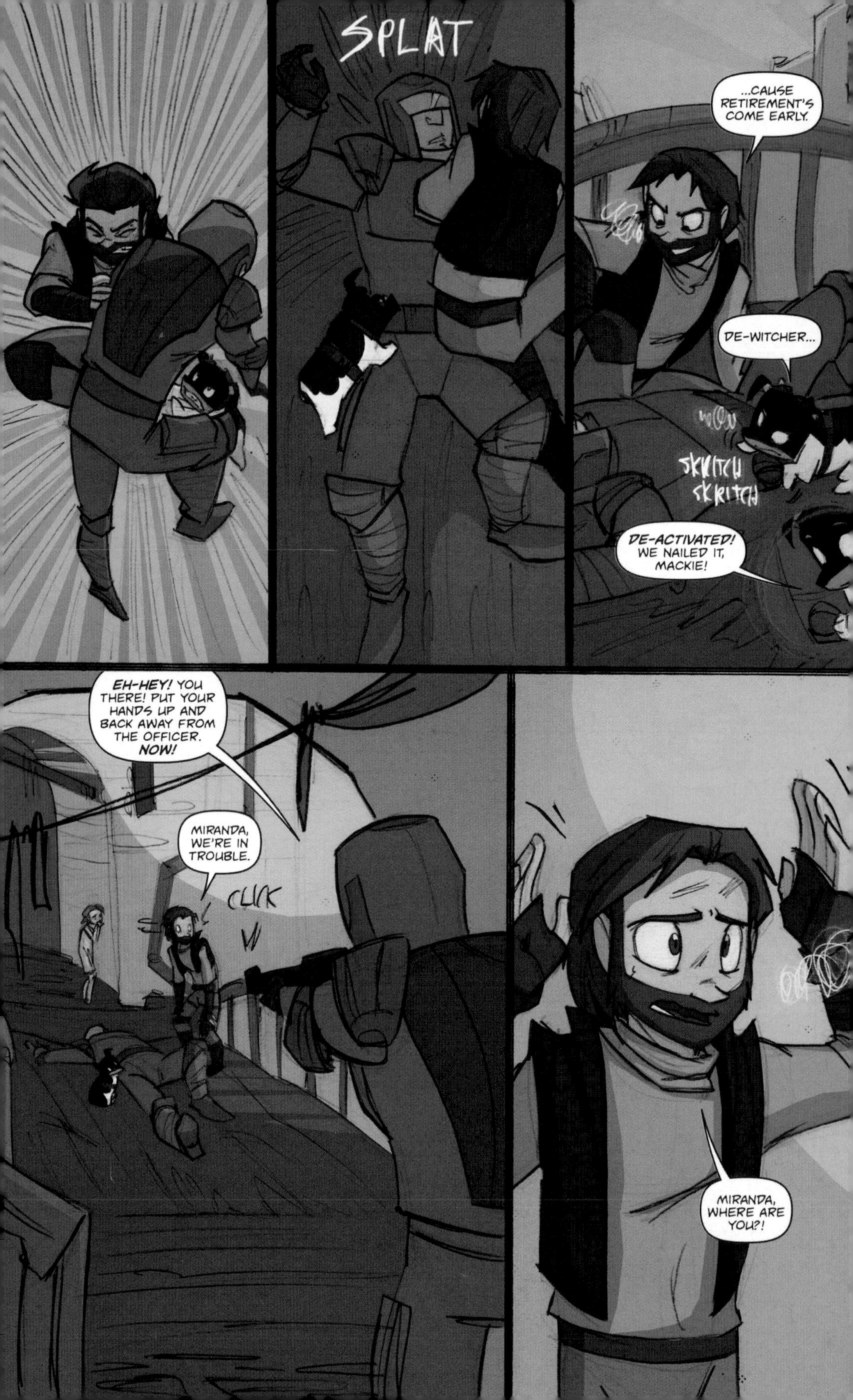
SPLAT
...CAUSE RETIREMENT'S COME EARLY.
DE-WITCHER...
SKRITCH SKRITCH
DE-ACTIVATED! WE NAILED IT, MACKIE!
EH-HEY! YOU THERE! PUT YOUR HANDS UP AND BACK AWAY FROM THE OFFICER. NOW!
MIRANDA, WE'RE IN TROUBLE.
CLICK
MIRANDA, WHERE ARE YOU?!

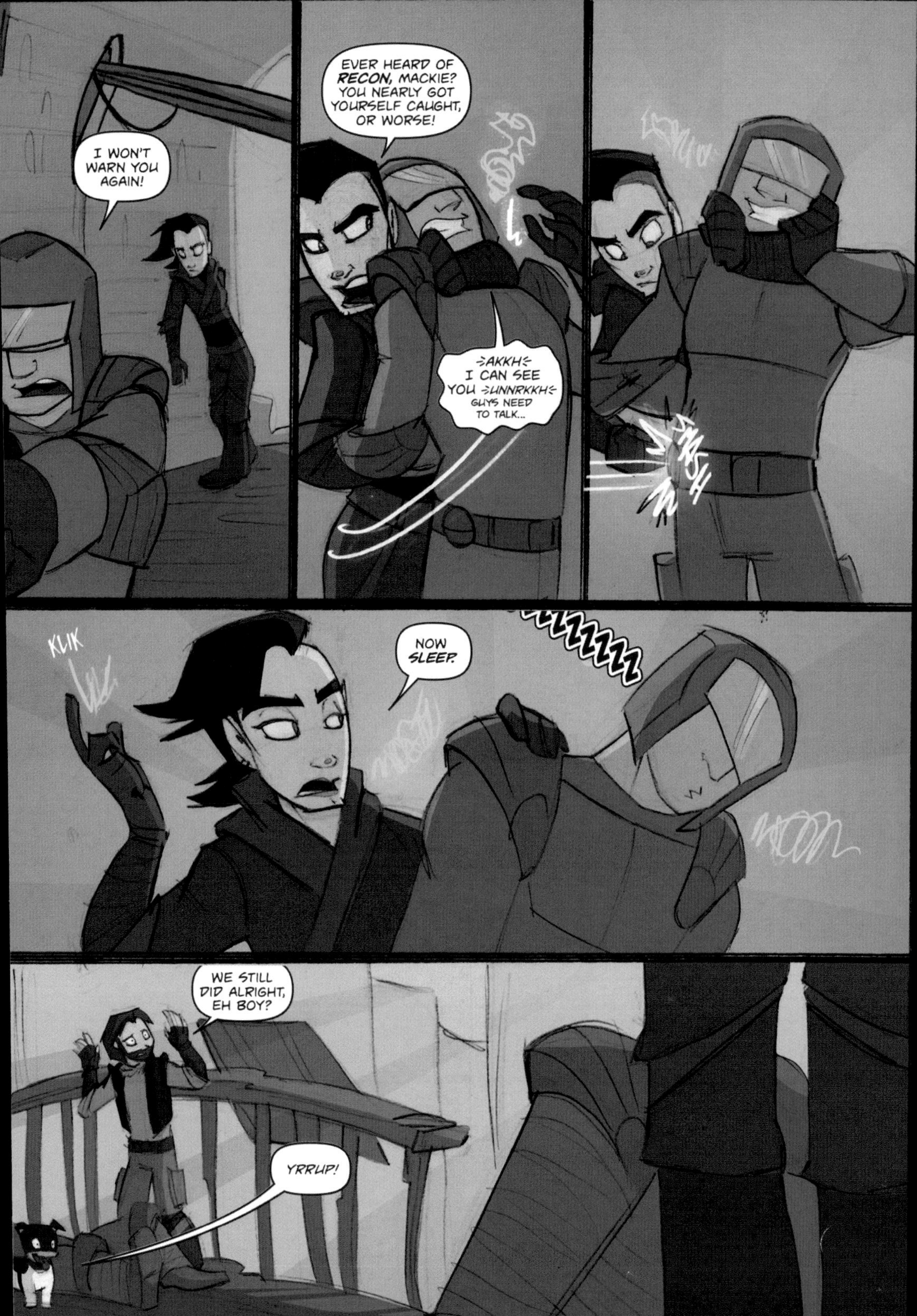
I WON'T WARN YOU AGAIN!
EVER HEARD OF RECON, MACKIE? YOU NEARLY GOT YOURSELF CAUGHT, OR WORSE!
=AKKH= I CAN SEE YOU =UNNRKKH= GUYS NEED TO TALK...
SMASH
KLIK
NOW SLEEP.
ZZZZZZZZ
WE STILL DID ALRIGHT, EH BOY?
YRRUP!

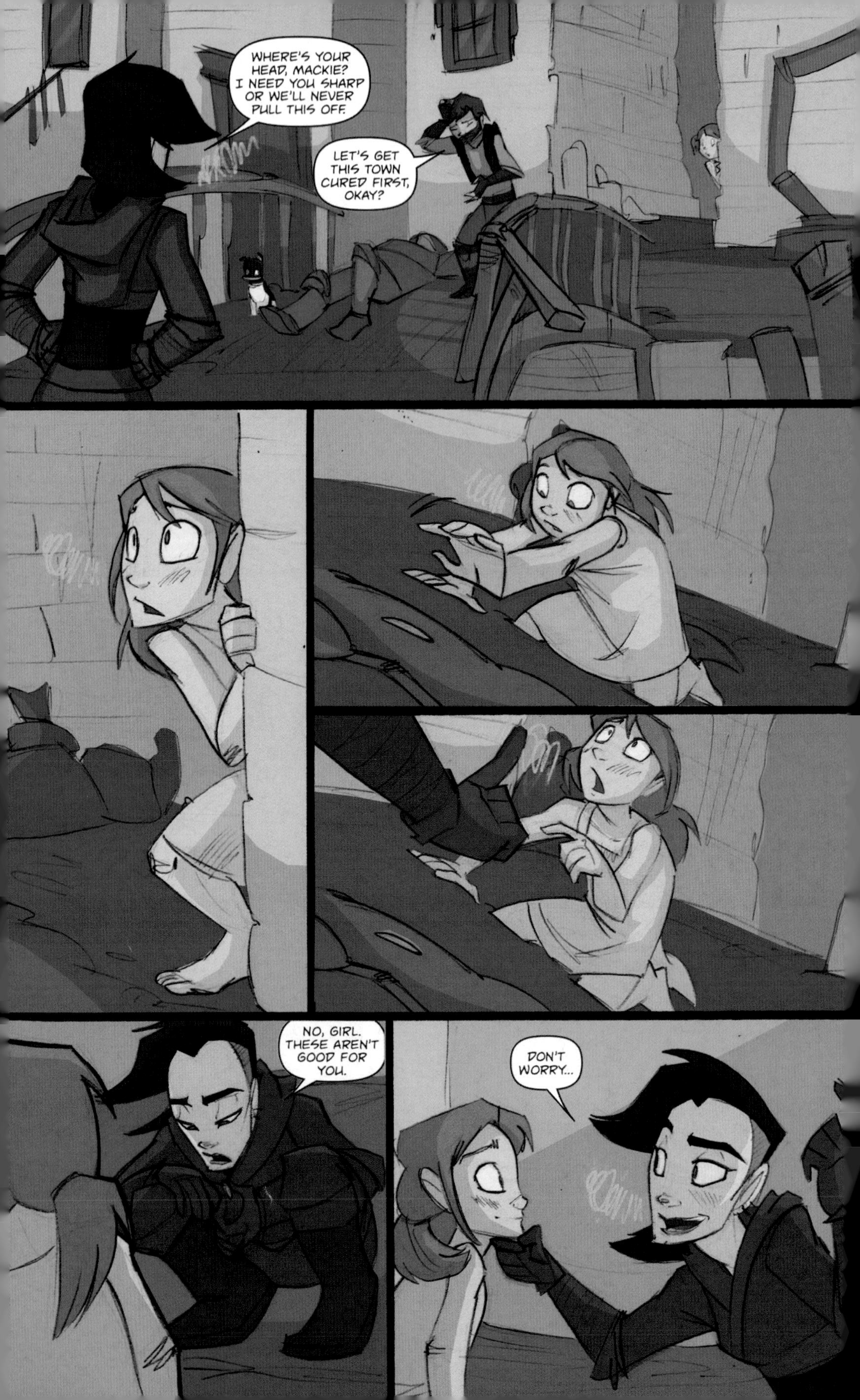

WHERE'S YOUR HEAD, MACKIE? I NEED YOU SHARP OR WE'LL NEVER PULL THIS OFF.
LET'S GET THIS TOWN CURED FIRST, OKAY?
NO, GIRL. THESE AREN'T GOOD FOR YOU.
DON'T WORRY...

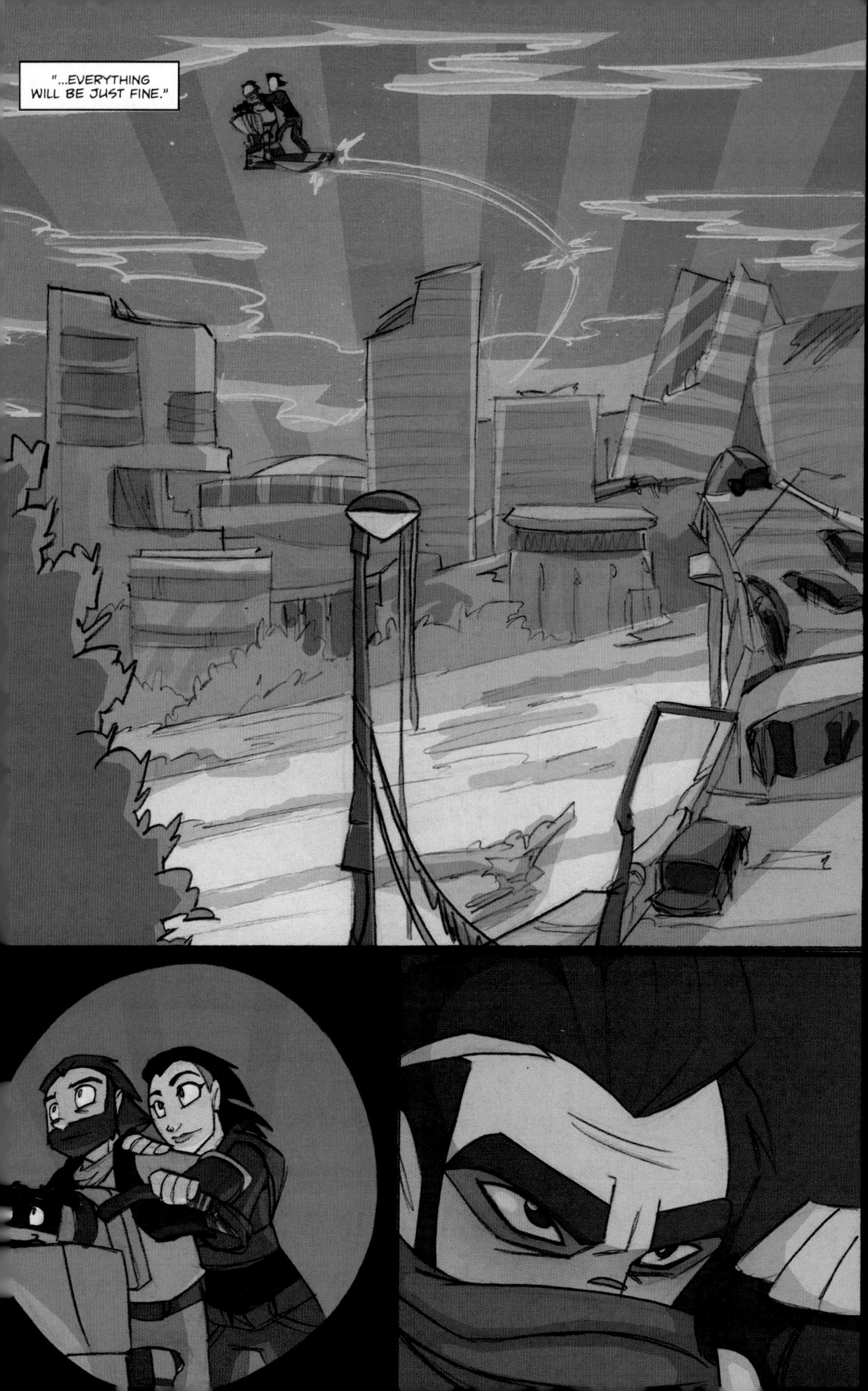
"...EVERYTHING WILL BE JUST FINE."

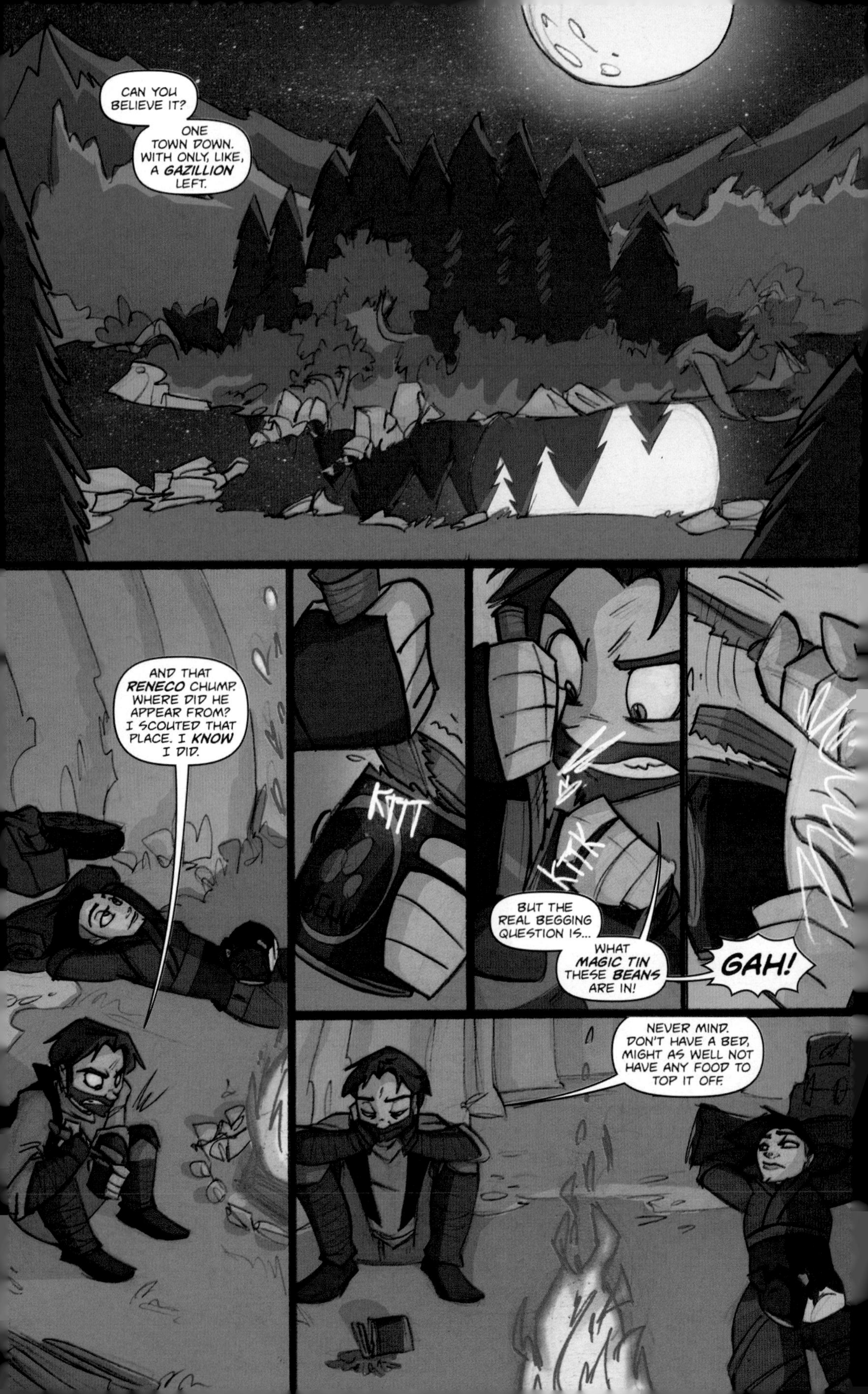
CAN YOU BELIEVE IT?
ONE TOWN DOWN. WITH ONLY, LIKE, A GAZILLION LEFT.
AND THAT RENECO CHUMP. WHERE DID HE APPEAR FROM? I SCOUTED THAT PLACE. I KNOW I DID.
KTTT
KTTK
BUT THE REAL BEGGING QUESTION IS...
WHAT MAGIC TIN THESE BEANS ARE IN!
GAH!
NEVER MIND. DON'T HAVE A BED, MIGHT AS WELL NOT HAVE ANY FOOD TO TOP IT OFF.

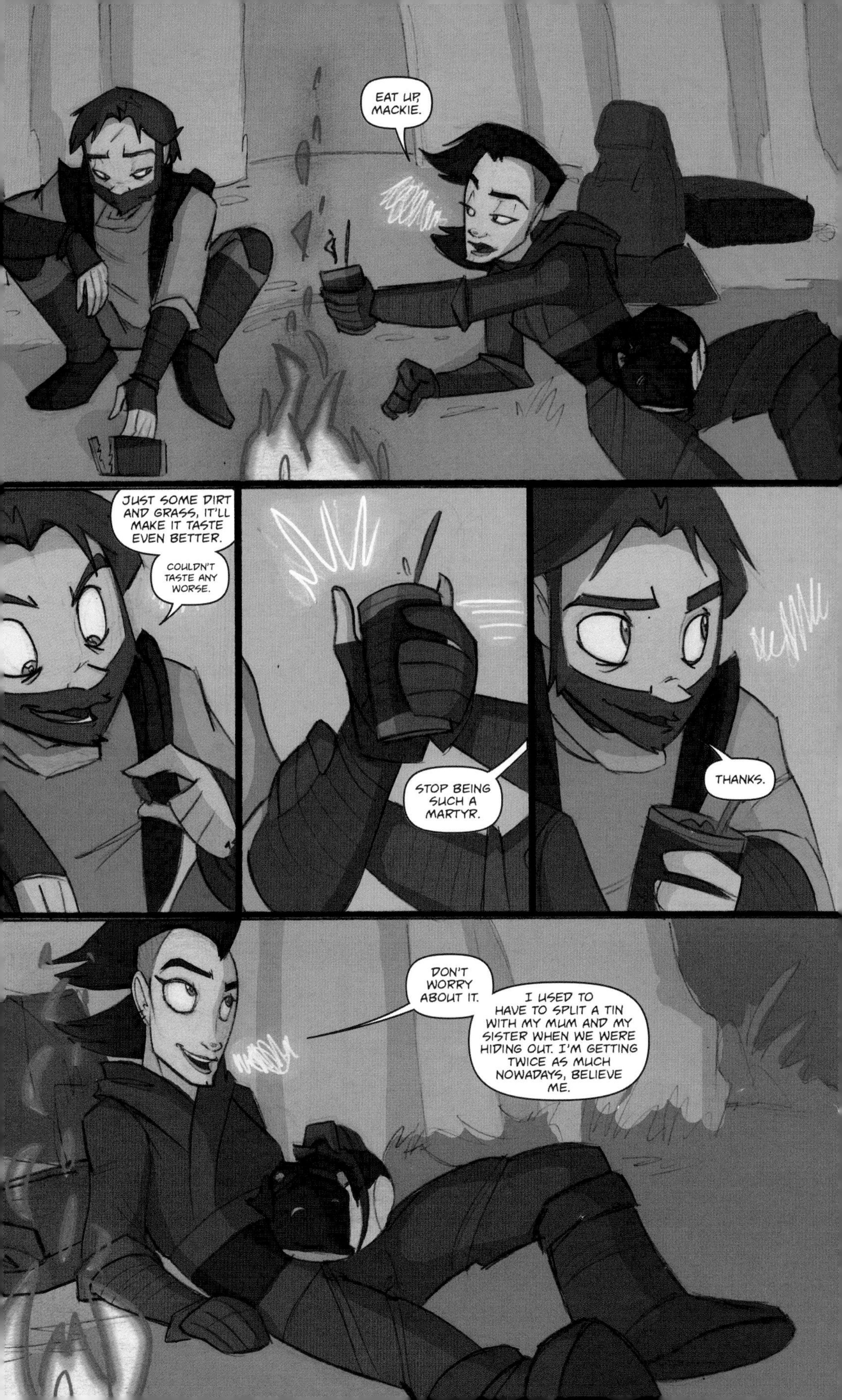
EAT UP, MACKIE.
JUST SOME DIRT AND GRASS, IT'LL MAKE IT TASTE EVEN BETTER.
COULDN'T TASTE ANY WORSE.
STOP BEING SUCH A MARTYR.
THANKS.
DON'T WORRY ABOUT IT.
I USED TO HAVE TO SPLIT A TIN WITH MY MUM AND MY SISTER WHEN WE WERE HIDING OUT. I'M GETTING TWICE AS MUCH NOWADAYS, BELIEVE ME.

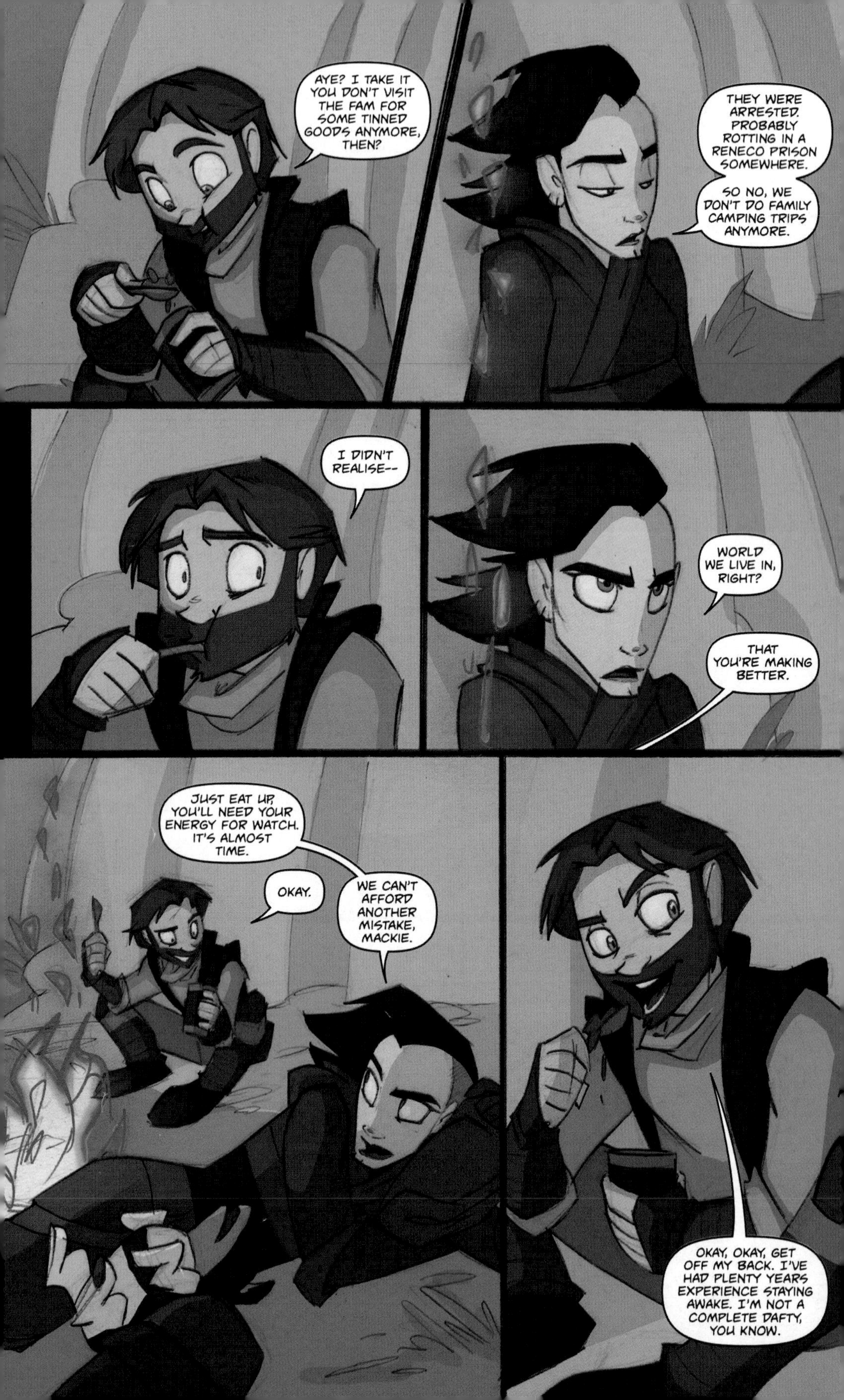
AYE? I TAKE IT YOU DON'T VISIT THE FAM FOR SOME TINNED GOODS ANYMORE, THEN?
THEY WERE ARRESTED. PROBABLY ROTTING IN A RENECO PRISON SOMEWHERE.
SO NO, WE DON'T DO FAMILY CAMPING TRIPS ANYMORE.
I DIDN'T REALISE--
WORLD WE LIVE IN, RIGHT?
THAT YOU'RE MAKING BETTER.
JUST EAT UP. YOU'LL NEED YOUR ENERGY FOR WATCH. IT'S ALMOST TIME.
OKAY.
WE CAN'T AFFORD ANOTHER MISTAKE, MACKIE.
OKAY, OKAY, GET OFF MY BACK. I'VE HAD PLENTY YEARS EXPERIENCE STAYING AWAKE. I'M NOT A COMPLETE DAFTY, YOU KNOW.

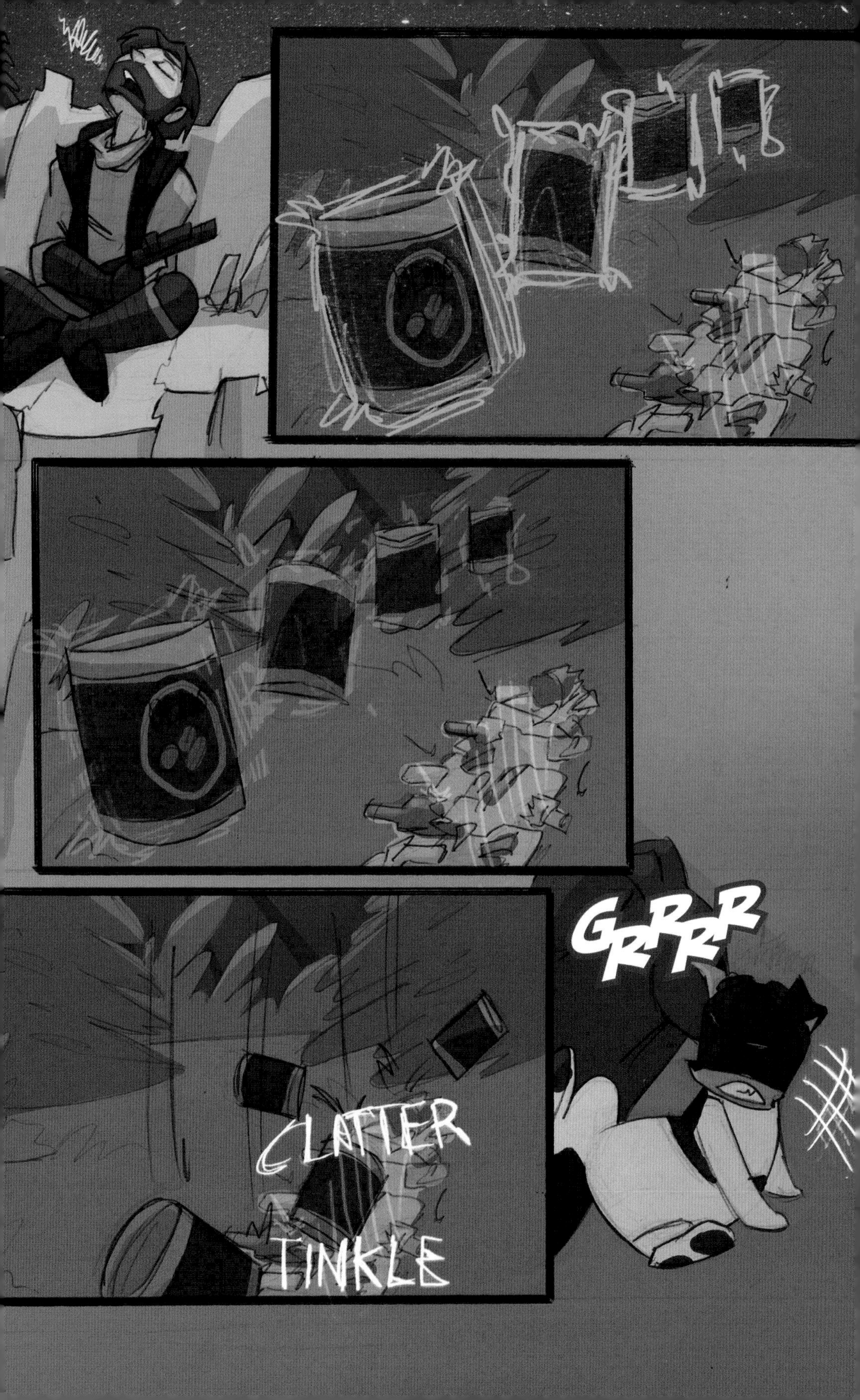
GRRRR
CLATTER
TINKLE

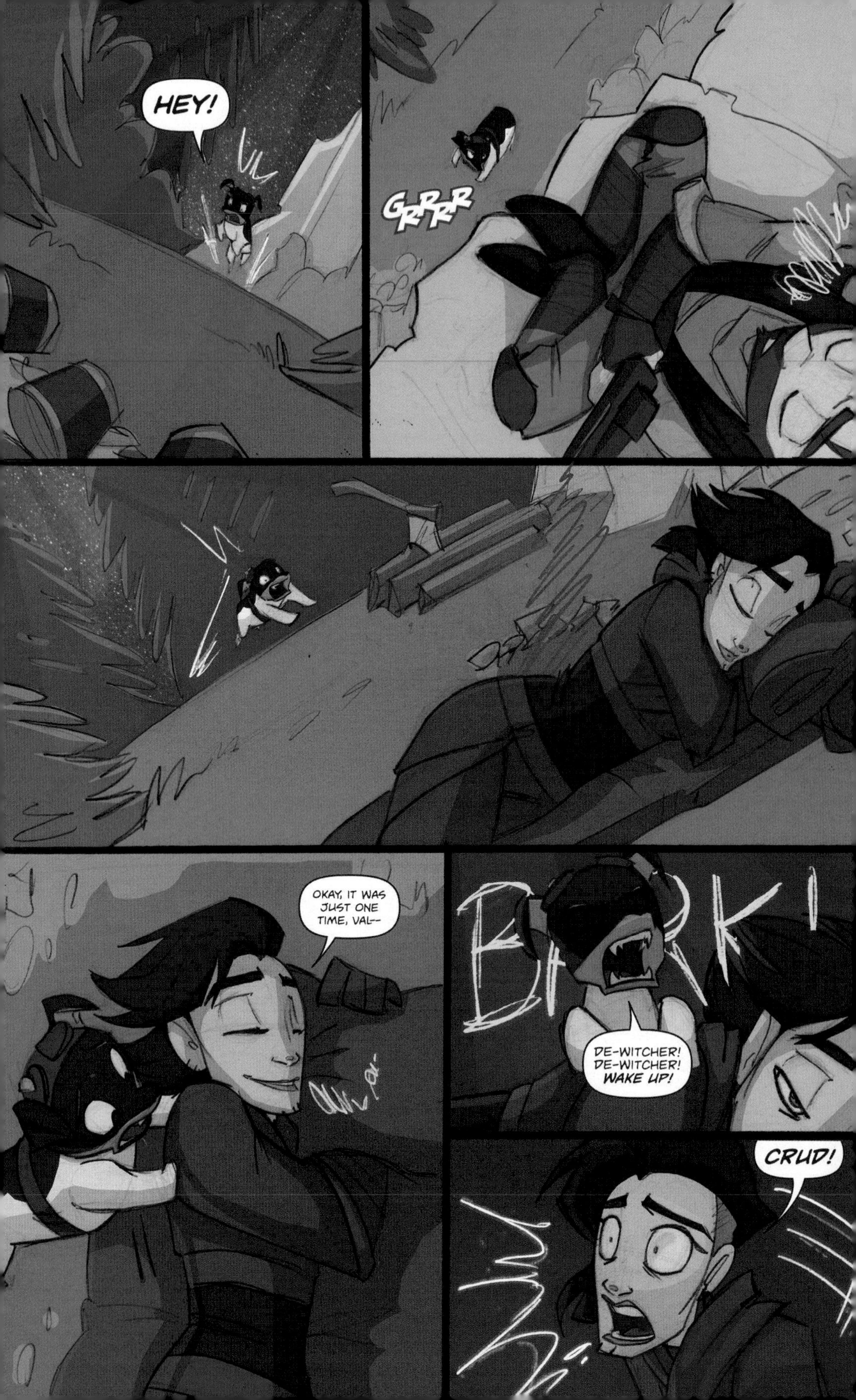
HEY!
GRRRR
OKAY, IT WAS JUST ONE TIME, VAL--
BARK!
DE-WITCHER! DE-WITCHER! WAKE UP!
CRUD!

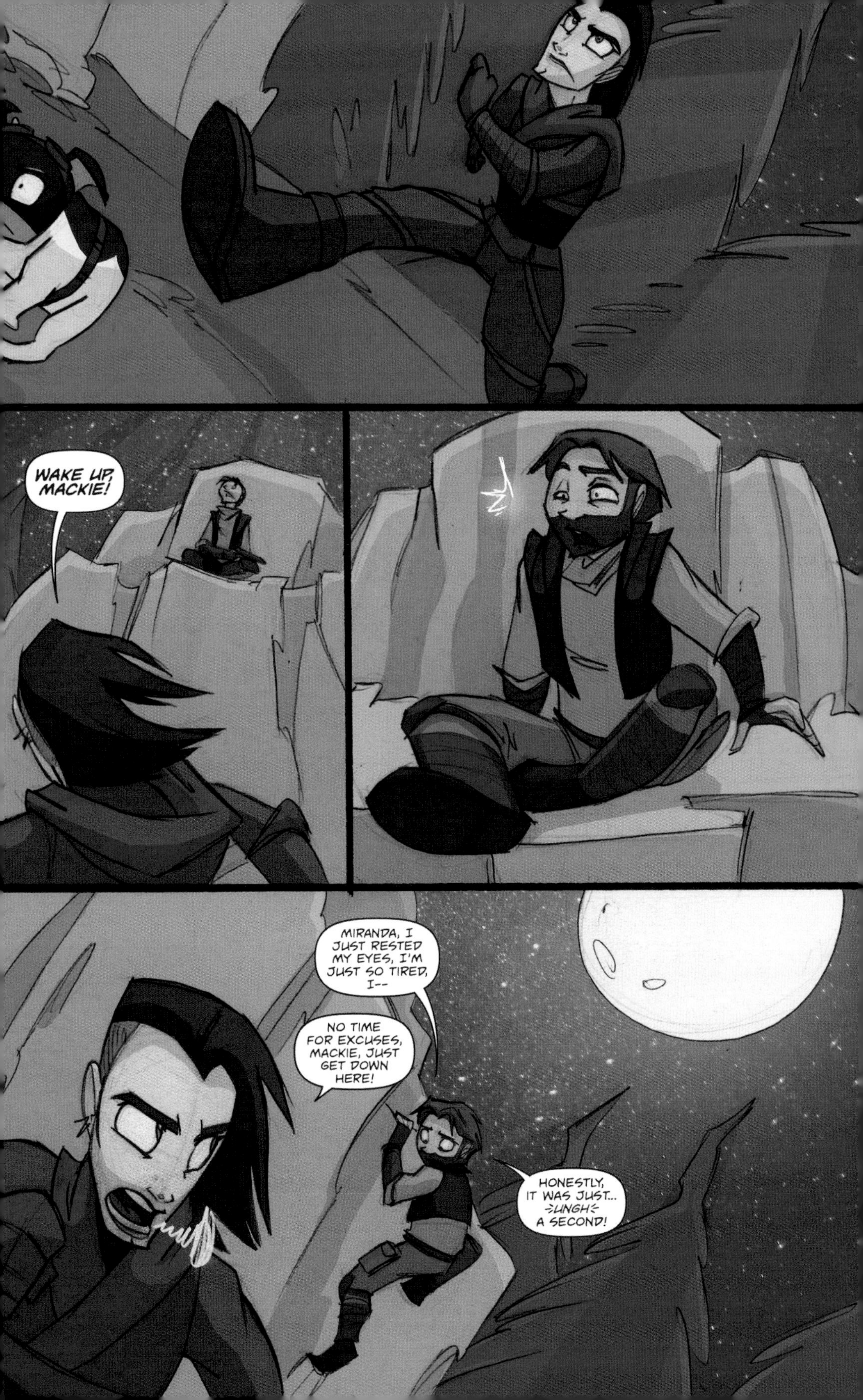

WAKE UP, MACKIE!
MIRANDA, I JUST RESTED MY EYES, I'M JUST SO TIRED, I--
NO TIME FOR EXCUSES, MACKIE, JUST GET DOWN HERE!
HONESTLY, IT WAS JUST... UNGH A SECOND!

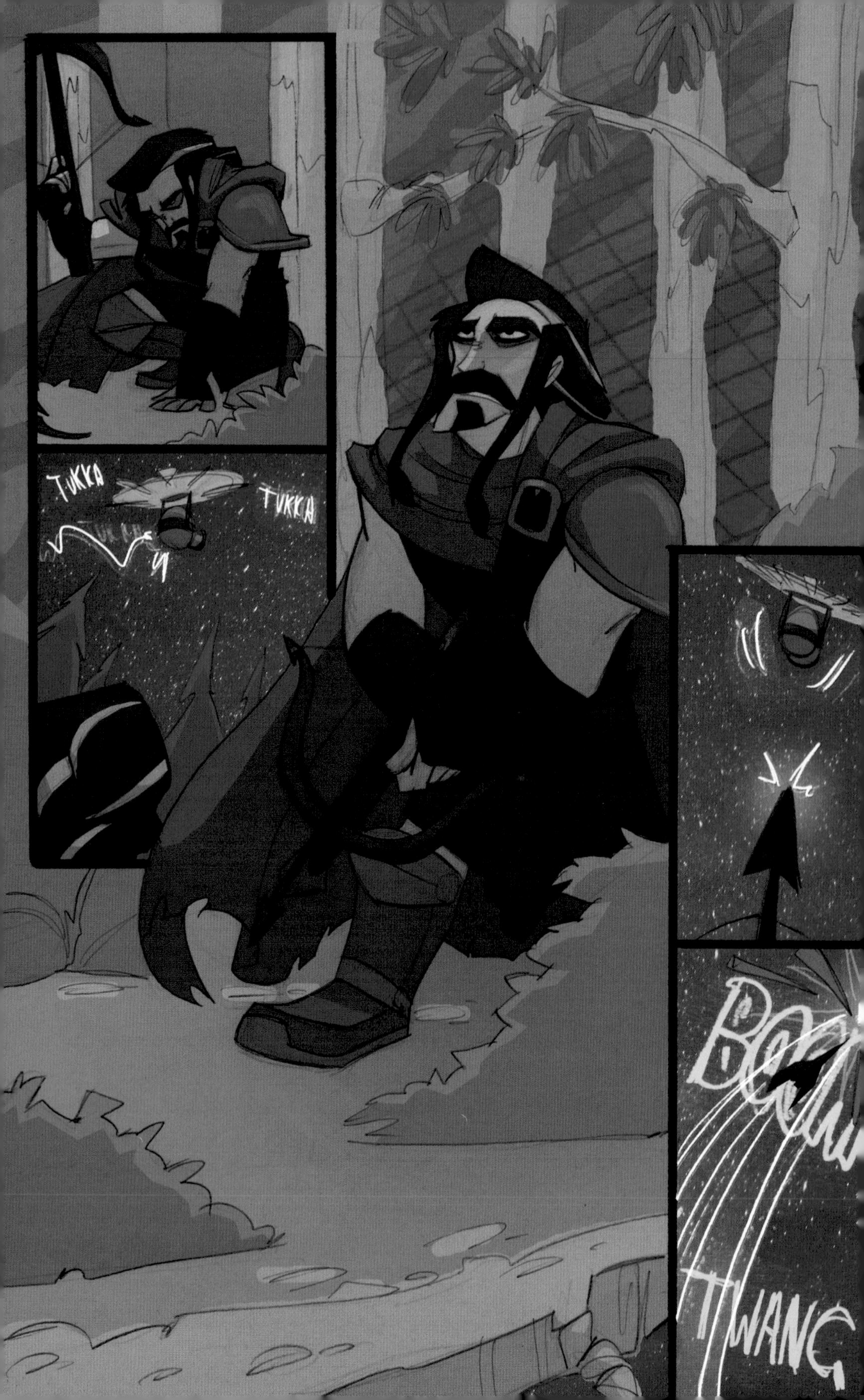
TUKKA
TUKKA
TWANG

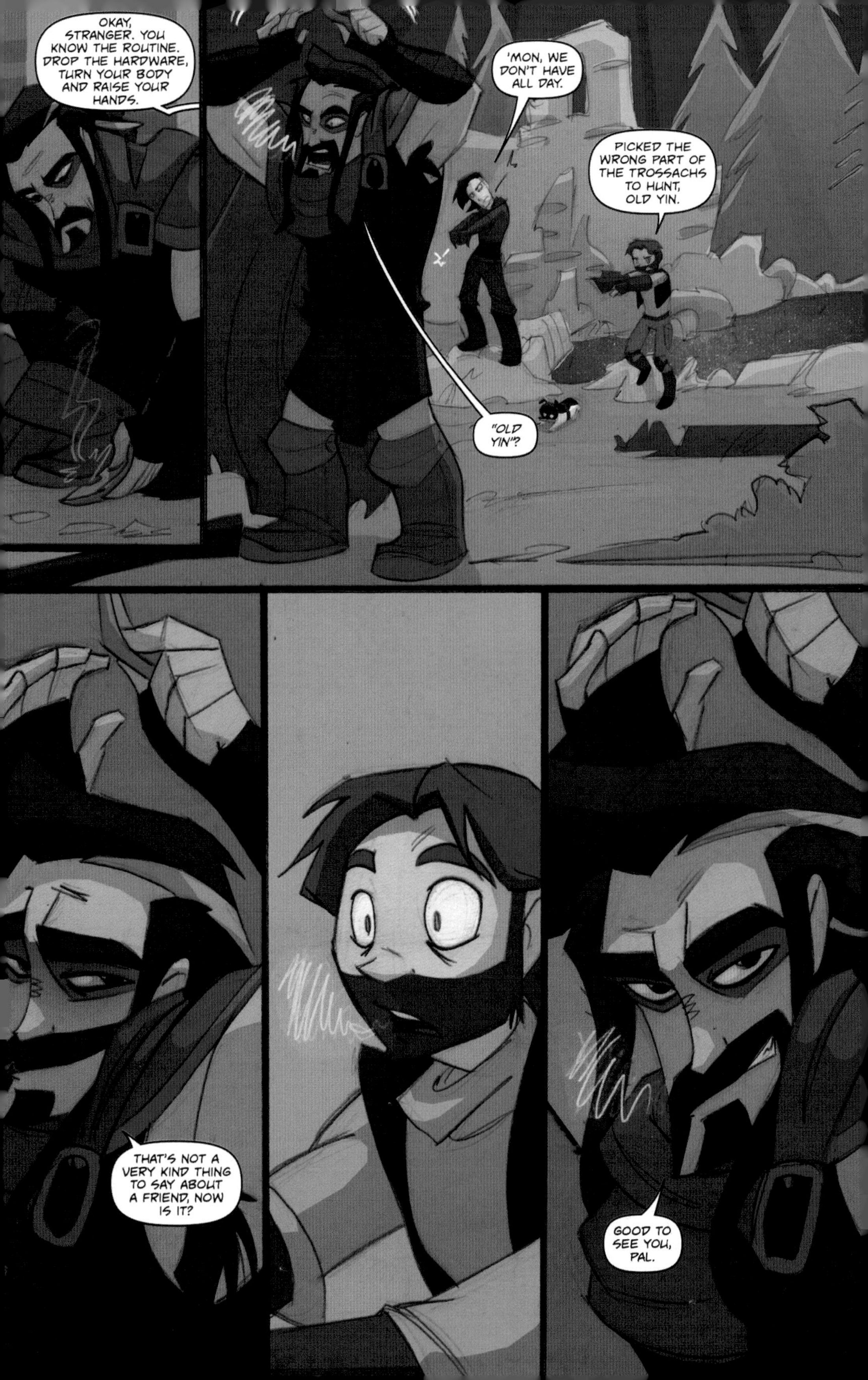
OKAY, STRANGER. YOU KNOW THE ROUTINE. DROP THE HARDWARE, TURN YOUR BODY AND RAISE YOUR HANDS.
'MON, WE DON'T HAVE ALL DAY.
PICKED THE WRONG PART OF THE TROSSACHS TO HUNT, OLD YIN.
"OLD YIN"?
THAT'S NOT A VERY KIND THING TO SAY ABOUT A FRIEND, NOW IS IT?
GOOD TO SEE YOU, PAL.

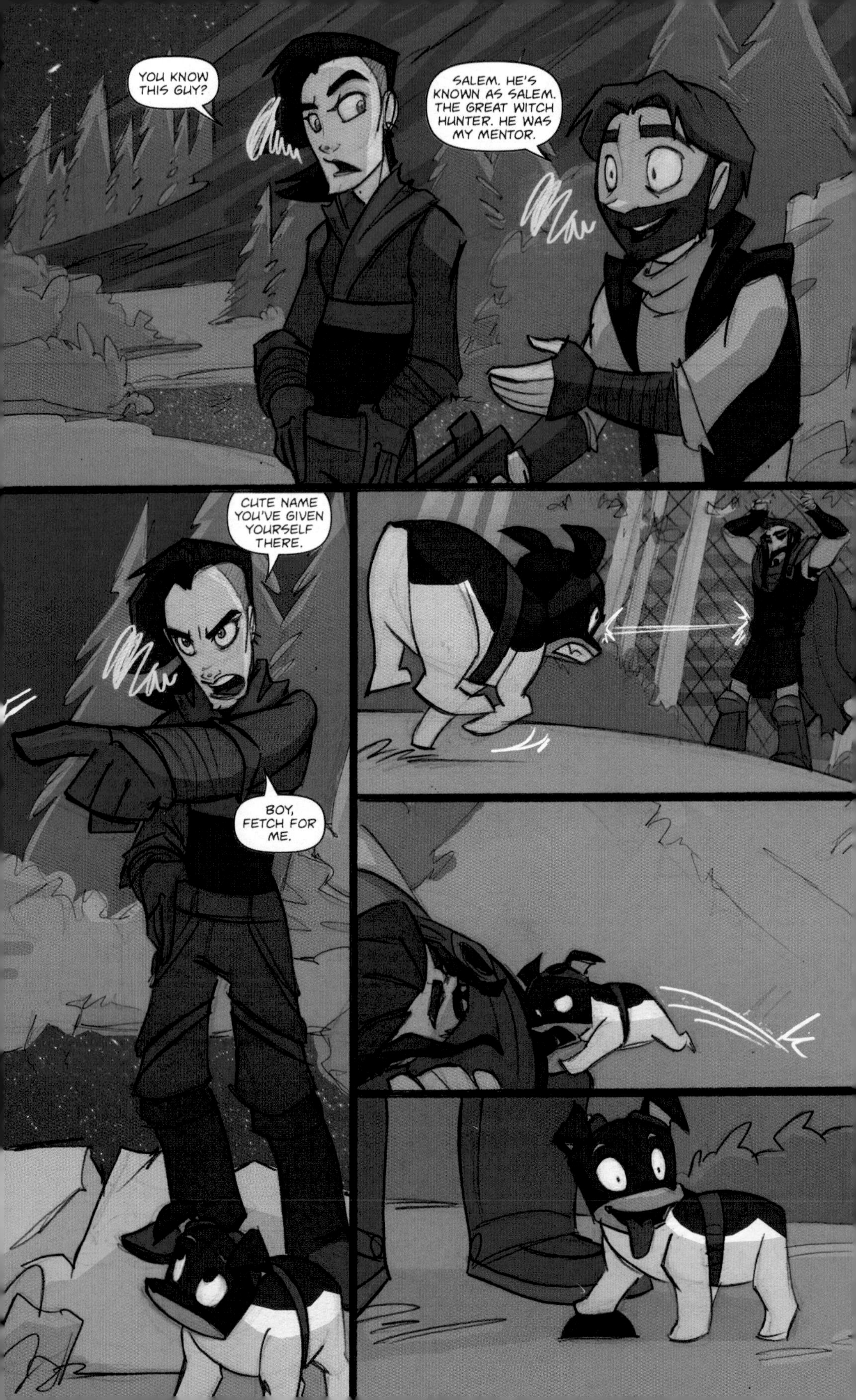
YOU KNOW THIS GUY?
SALEM. HE'S KNOWN AS SALEM. THE GREAT WITCH HUNTER. HE WAS MY MENTOR.
CUTE NAME YOU'VE GIVEN YOURSELF THERE.
BOY, FETCH FOR ME.

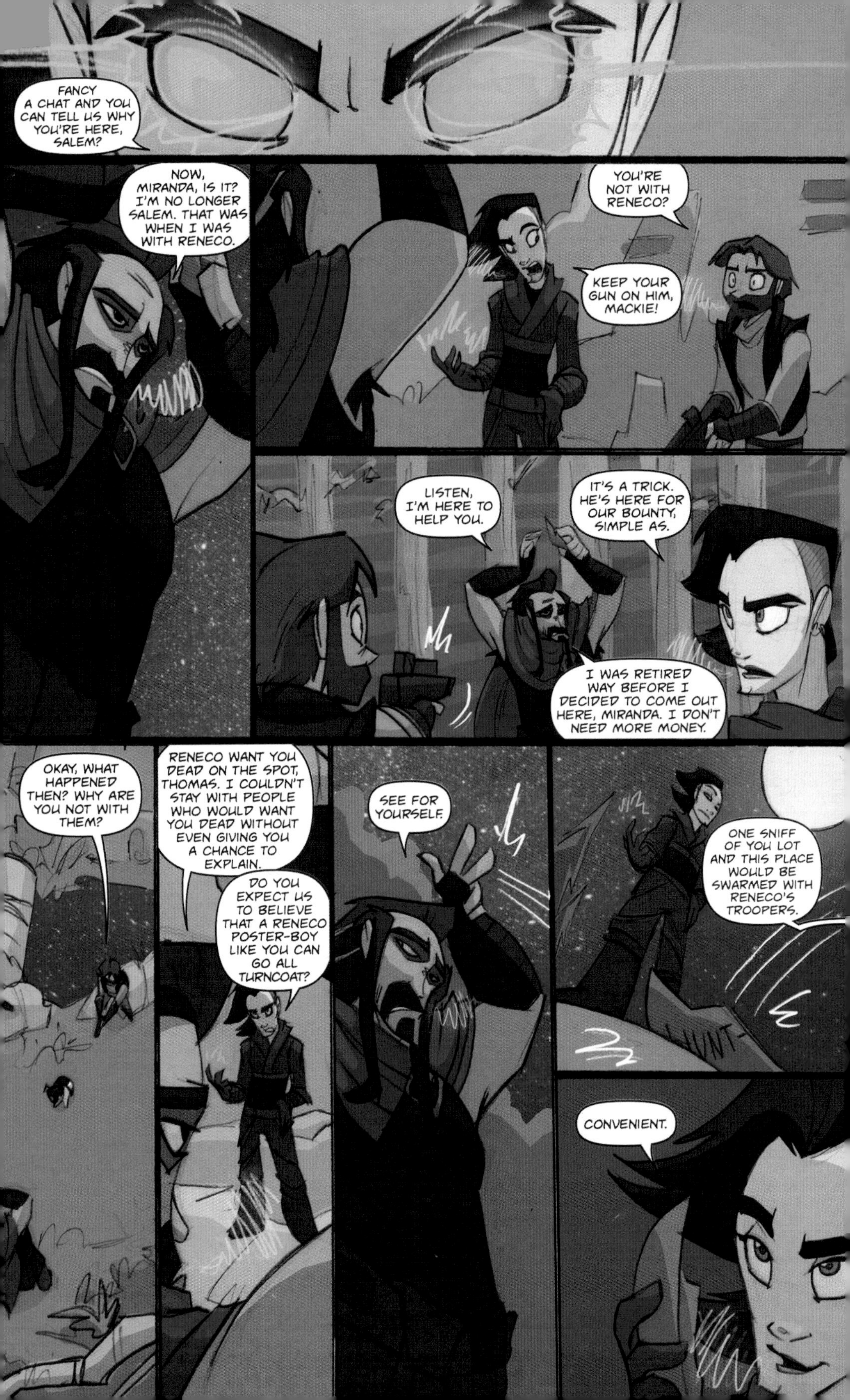
FANCY A CHAT AND YOU CAN TELL US WHY YOU'RE HERE, SALEM?
NOW, MIRANDA, IS IT? I'M NO LONGER SALEM. THAT WAS WHEN I WAS WITH RENECO.
YOU'RE NOT WITH RENECO?
KEEP YOUR GUN ON HIM, MACKIE!
LISTEN, I'M HERE TO HELP YOU.
IT'S A TRICK. HE'S HERE FOR OUR BOUNTY, SIMPLE AS.
I WAS RETIRED WAY BEFORE I DECIDED TO COME OUT HERE, MIRANDA. I DON'T NEED MORE MONEY.
OKAY, WHAT HAPPENED THEN? WHY ARE YOU NOT WITH THEM?
RENECO WANT YOU DEAD ON THE SPOT, THOMAS. I COULDN'T STAY WITH PEOPLE WHO WOULD WANT YOU DEAD WITHOUT EVEN GIVING YOU A CHANCE TO EXPLAIN.
DO YOU EXPECT US TO BELIEVE THAT A RENECO POSTER-BOY LIKE YOU CAN GO ALL TURNCOAT?
SEE FOR YOURSELF.
ONE SNIFF OF YOU LOT AND THIS PLACE WOULD BE SWARMED WITH RENECO'S TROOPERS.
CONVENIENT.

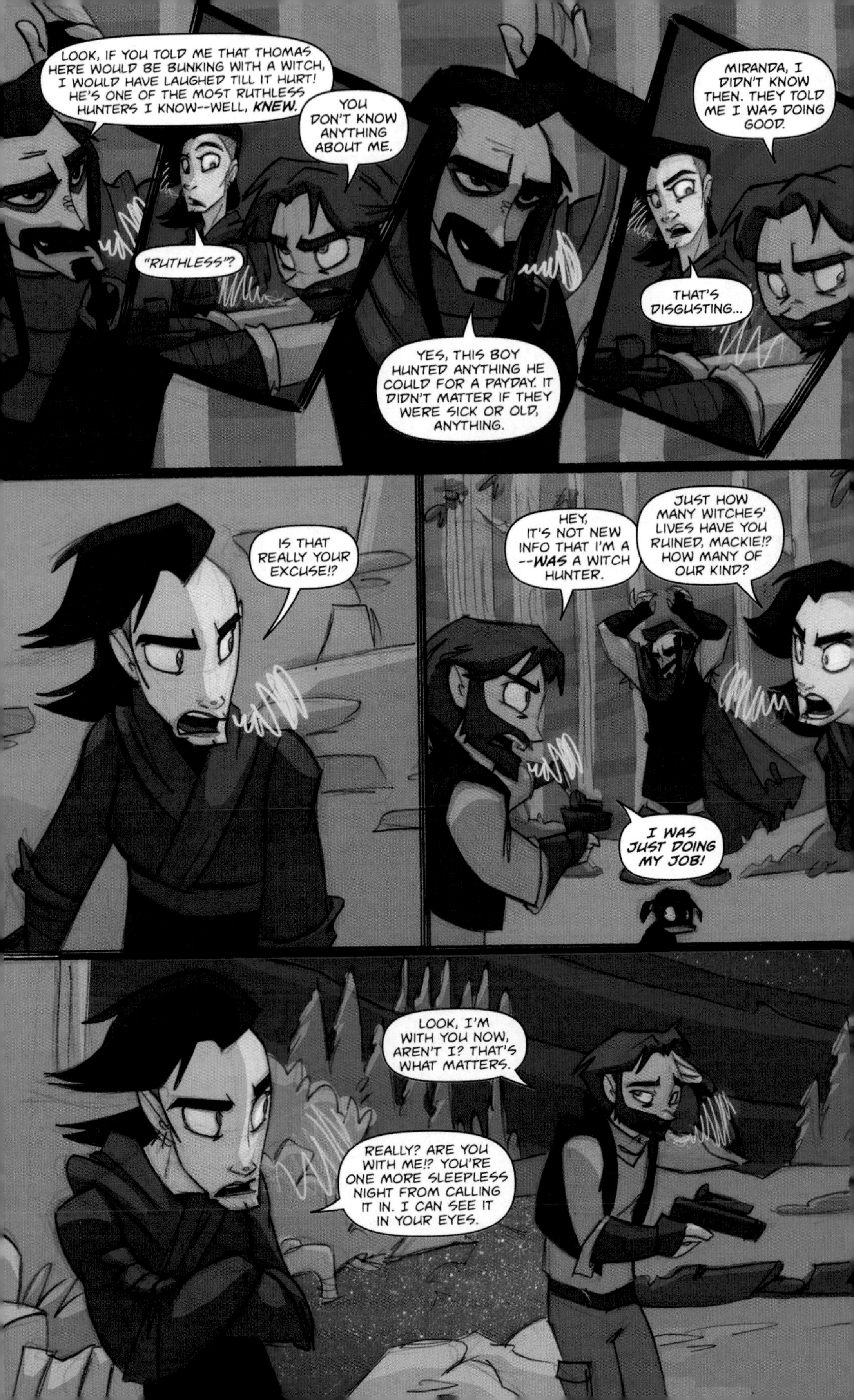
LOOK, IF YOU TOLD ME THAT THOMAS HERE WOULD BE BUNKING WITH A WITCH, I WOULD HAVE LAUGHED TILL IT HURT! HE'S ONE OF THE MOST RUTHLESS HUNTERS I KNOW--WELL, **KNEW.**
"RUTHLESS"?
YOU DON'T KNOW ANYTHING ABOUT ME.
YES, THIS BOY HUNTED ANYTHING HE COULD FOR A PAYDAY. IT DIDN'T MATTER IF THEY WERE SICK OR OLD, ANYTHING.
MIRANDA, I DIDN'T KNOW THEN. THEY TOLD ME I WAS DOING GOOD.
THAT'S DISGUSTING...
IS THAT REALLY YOUR EXCUSE!?
HEY, IT'S NOT NEW INFO THAT I'M A --**WAS** A WITCH HUNTER.
JUST HOW MANY WITCHES' LIVES HAVE YOU RUINED, MACKIE!? HOW MANY OF OUR KIND?
I WAS JUST DOING MY JOB!
LOOK, I'M WITH YOU NOW, AREN'T I? THAT'S WHAT MATTERS.
REALLY? ARE YOU WITH ME!? YOU'RE ONE MORE SLEEPLESS NIGHT FROM CALLING IT IN. I CAN SEE IT IN YOUR EYES.

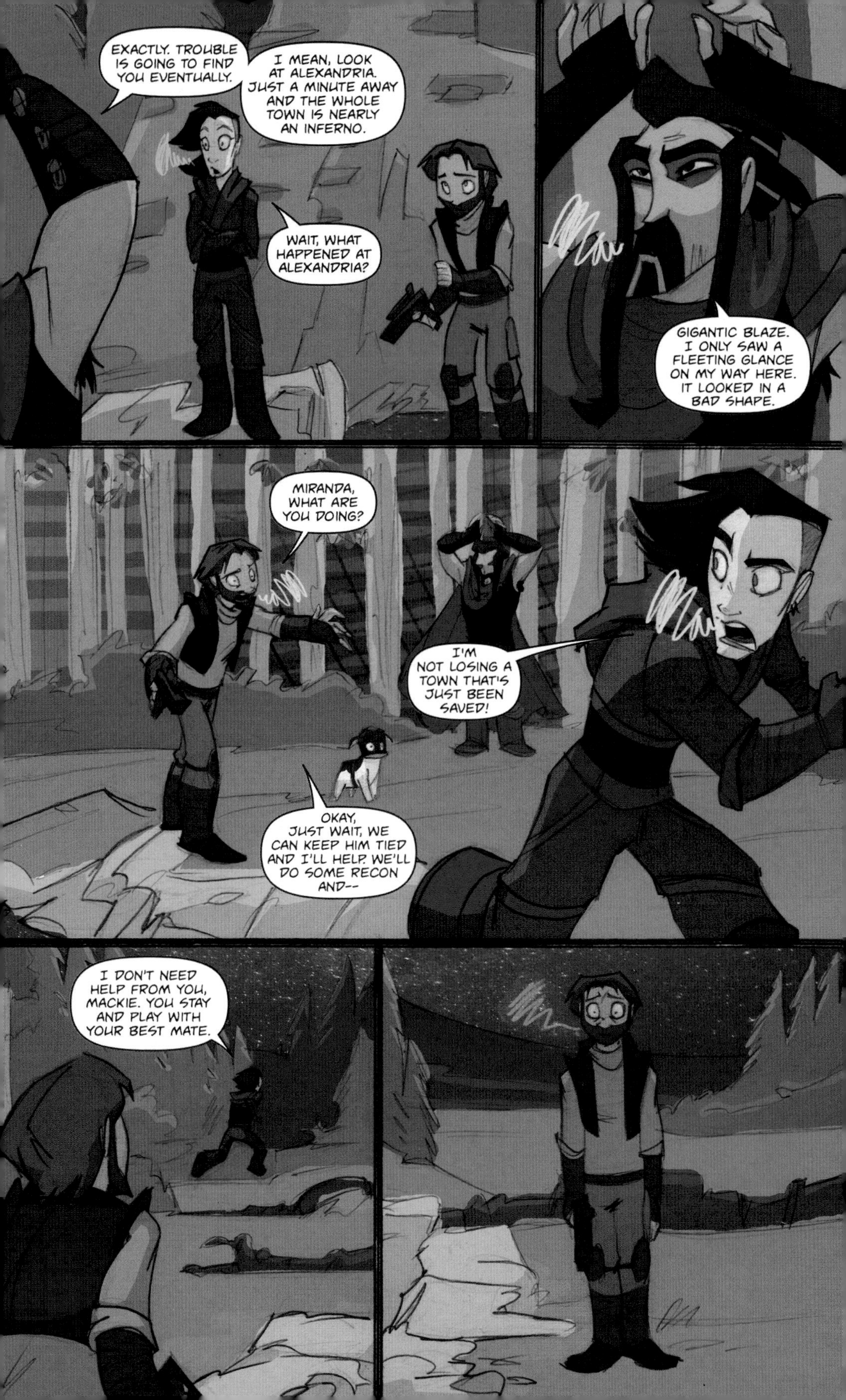
EXACTLY. TROUBLE IS GOING TO FIND YOU EVENTUALLY.
I MEAN, LOOK AT ALEXANDRIA. JUST A MINUTE AWAY AND THE WHOLE TOWN IS NEARLY AN INFERNO.
WAIT, WHAT HAPPENED AT ALEXANDRIA?
GIGANTIC BLAZE. I ONLY SAW A FLEETING GLANCE ON MY WAY HERE. IT LOOKED IN A BAD SHAPE.
MIRANDA, WHAT ARE YOU DOING?
I'M NOT LOSING A TOWN THAT'S JUST BEEN SAVED!
OKAY, JUST WAIT, WE CAN KEEP HIM TIED AND I'LL HELP. WE'LL DO SOME RECON AND--
I DON'T NEED HELP FROM YOU, MACKIE. YOU STAY AND PLAY WITH YOUR BEST MATE.

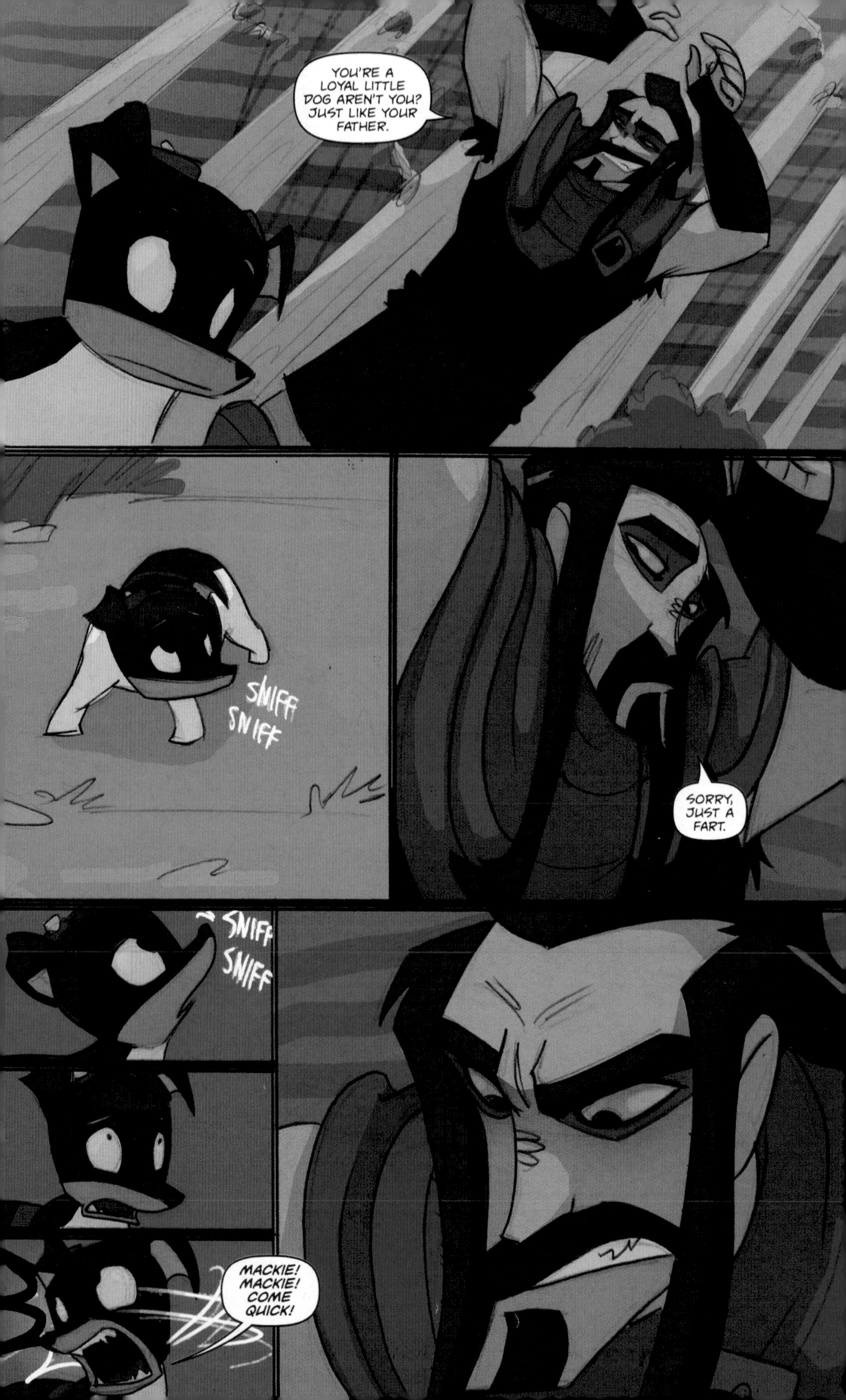
YOU'RE A LOYAL LITTLE DOG AREN'T YOU? JUST LIKE YOUR FATHER.
SNIFF SNIFF
SORRY, JUST A FART.
SNIFF SNIFF
MACKIE! MACKIE! COME QUICK!

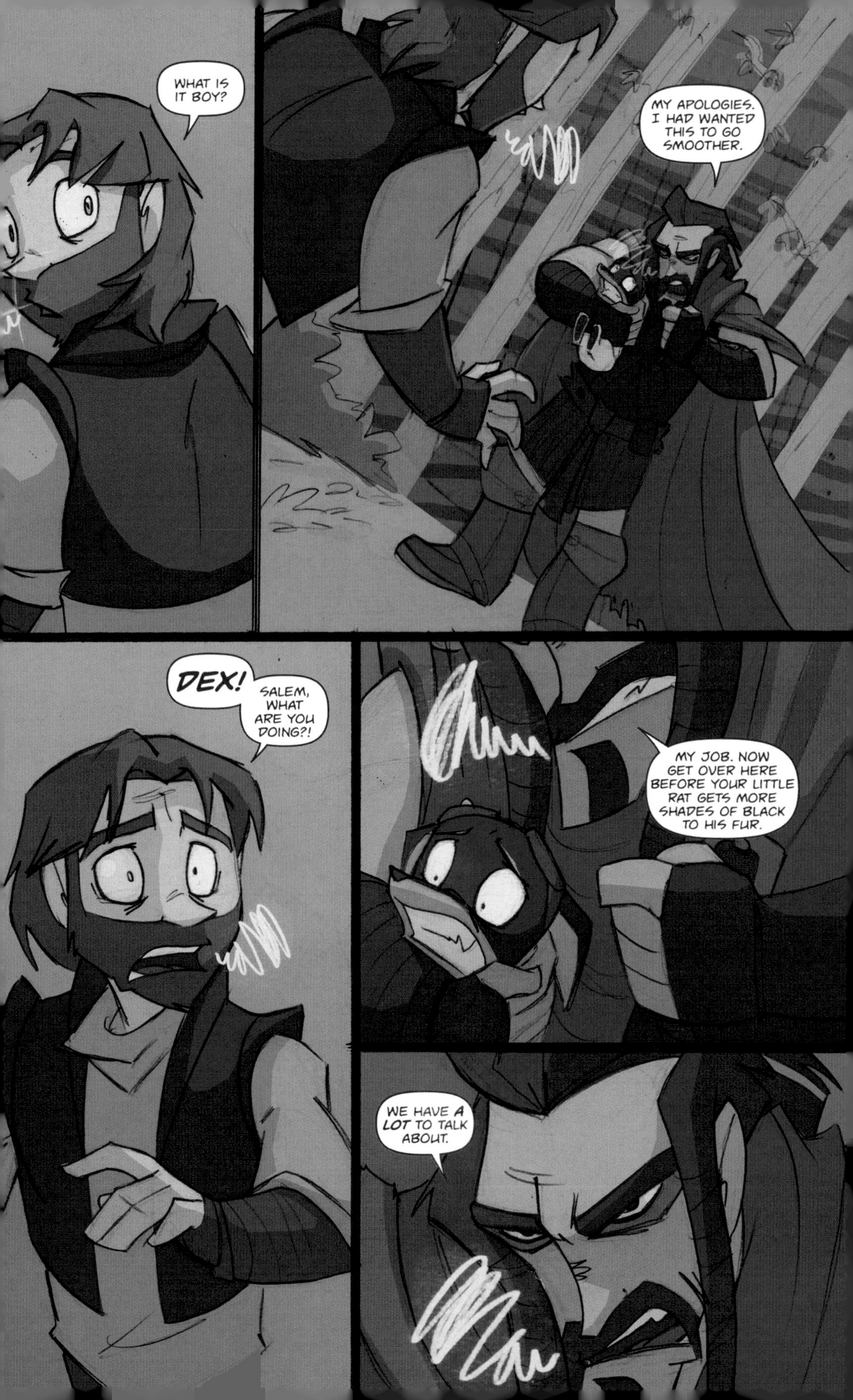
WHAT IS IT BOY?
MY APOLOGIES. I HAD WANTED THIS TO GO SMOOTHER.
DEX!
SALEM, WHAT ARE YOU DOING?!
MY JOB. NOW GET OVER HERE BEFORE YOUR LITTLE RAT GETS MORE SHADES OF BLACK TO HIS FUR.
WE HAVE A LOT TO TALK ABOUT.

CHAPTER THREE

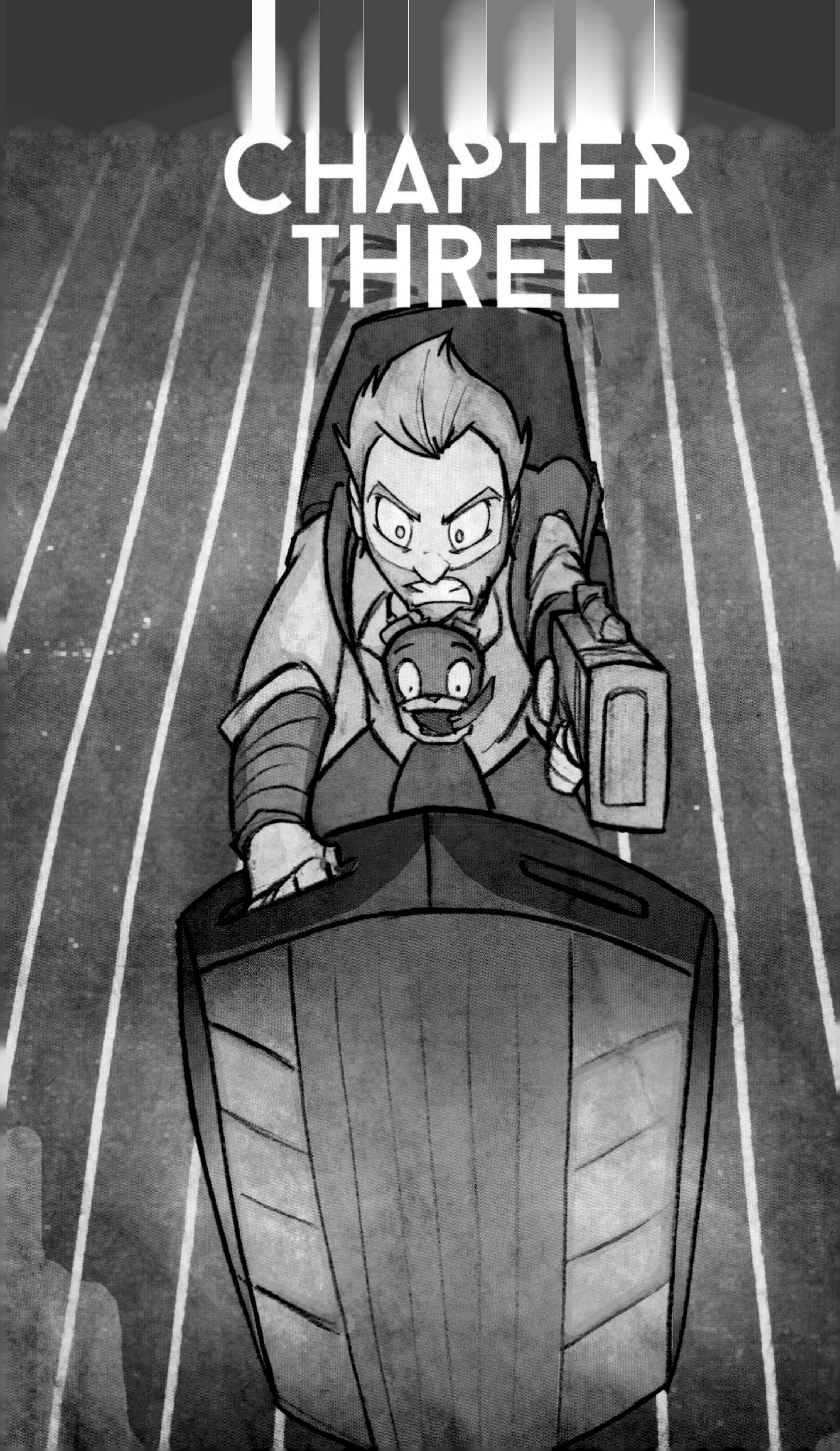

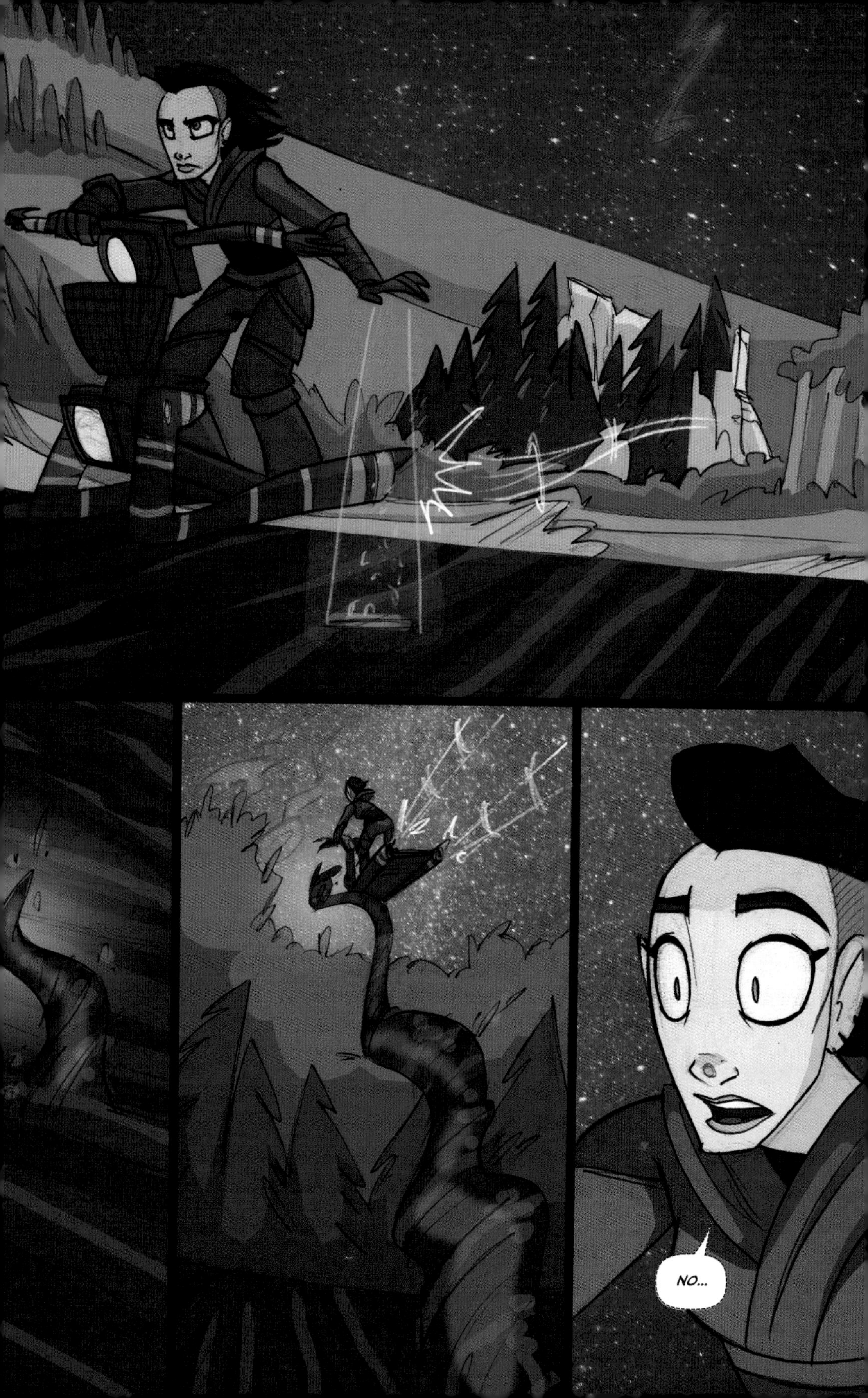
NO...

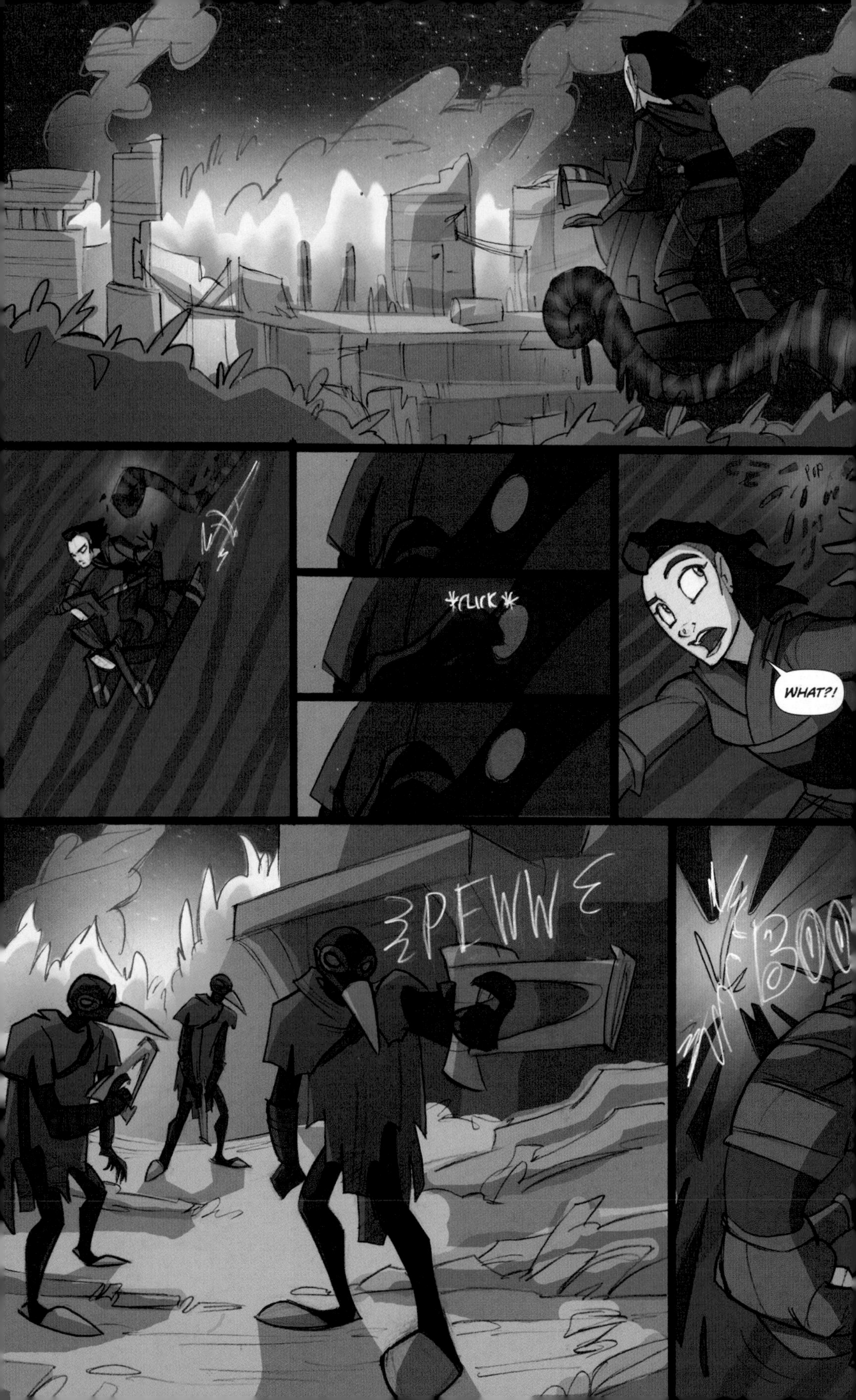
CLICK
POP
WHAT?!
PEWW
BOO

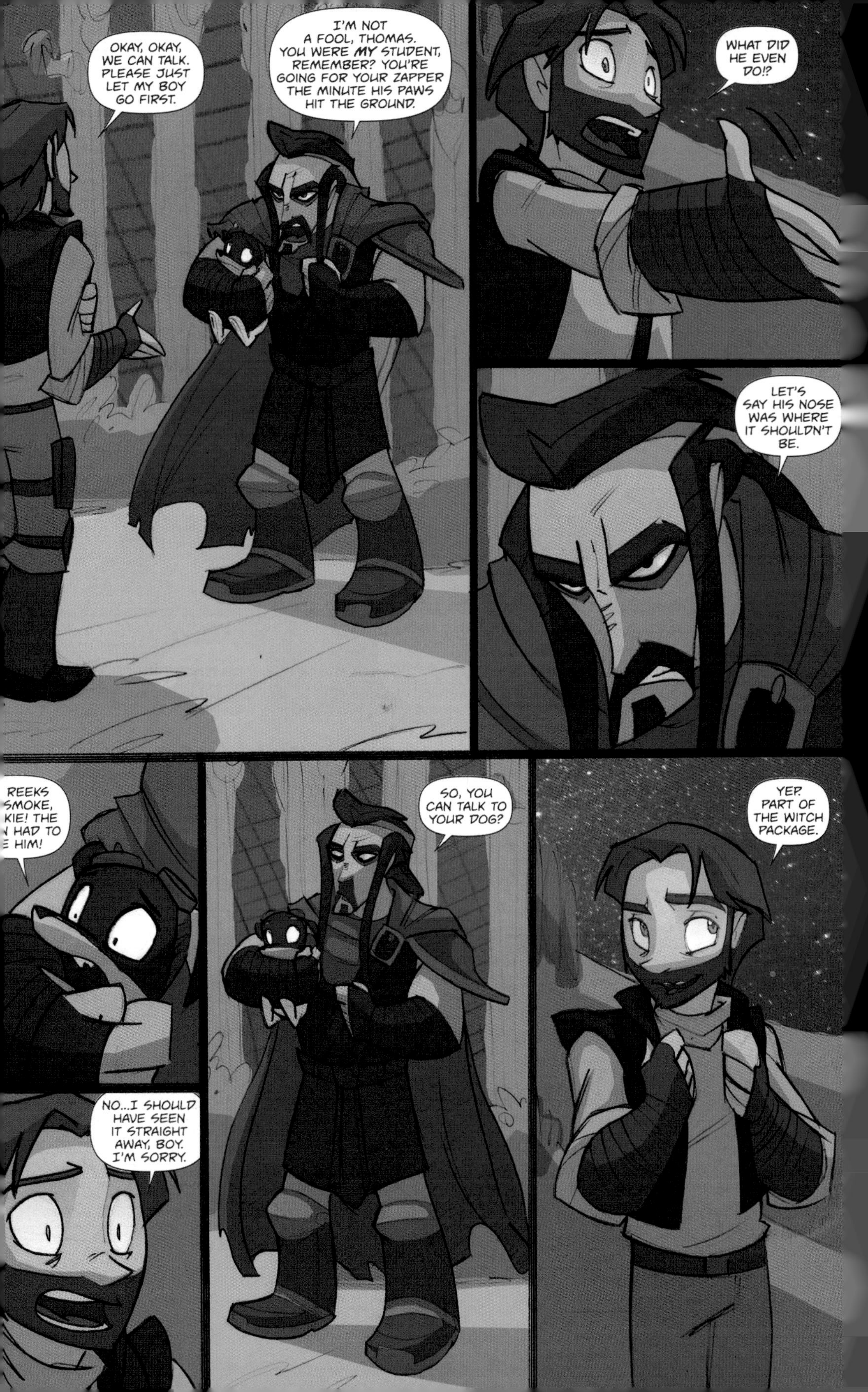
OKAY, OKAY, WE CAN TALK. PLEASE JUST LET MY BOY GO FIRST.
I'M NOT A FOOL, THOMAS. YOU WERE MY STUDENT, REMEMBER? YOU'RE GOING FOR YOUR ZAPPER THE MINUTE HIS PAWS HIT THE GROUND.
WHAT DID HE EVEN DO!?
LET'S SAY HIS NOSE WAS WHERE IT SHOULDN'T BE.
REEKS SMOKE, KIE! THE HAD TO HIM!
NO...I SHOULD HAVE SEEN IT STRAIGHT AWAY, BOY. I'M SORRY.
SO, YOU CAN TALK TO YOUR DOG?
YEP. PART OF THE WITCH PACKAGE.

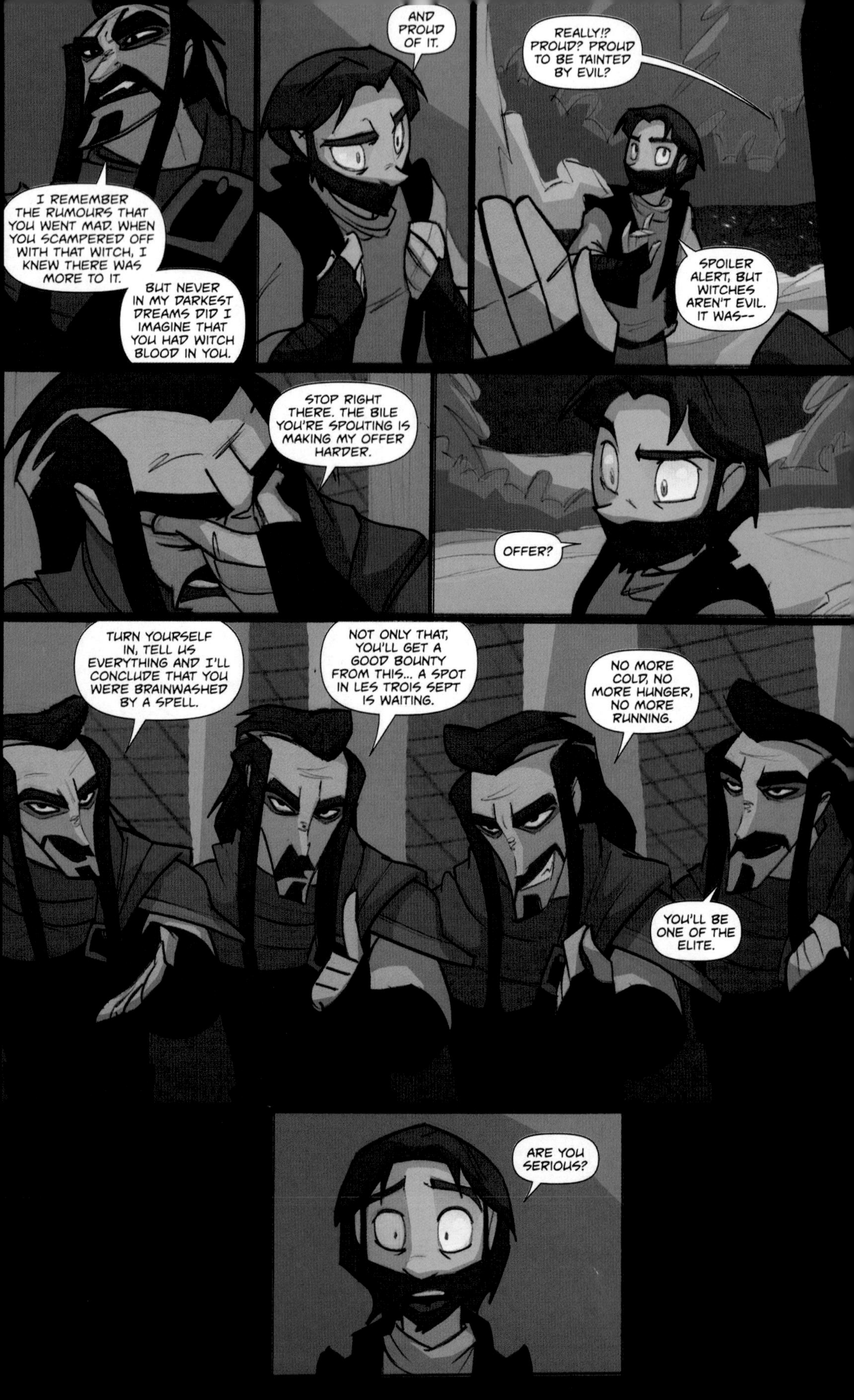
I REMEMBER THE RUMOURS THAT YOU WENT MAD. WHEN YOU SCAMPERED OFF WITH THAT WITCH, I KNEW THERE WAS MORE TO IT.
BUT NEVER IN MY DARKEST DREAMS DID I IMAGINE THAT YOU HAD WITCH BLOOD IN YOU.
AND PROUD OF IT.
REALLY!? PROUD? PROUD TO BE TAINTED BY EVIL?
SPOILER ALERT, BUT WITCHES AREN'T EVIL. IT WAS--
STOP RIGHT THERE. THE BILE YOU'RE SPOUTING IS MAKING MY OFFER HARDER.
OFFER?
TURN YOURSELF IN, TELL US EVERYTHING AND I'LL CONCLUDE THAT YOU WERE BRAINWASHED BY A SPELL.
NOT ONLY THAT, YOU'LL GET A GOOD BOUNTY FROM THIS... A SPOT IN LES TROIS SEPT IS WAITING.
NO MORE COLD, NO MORE HUNGER, NO MORE RUNNING.
YOU'LL BE ONE OF THE ELITE.
ARE YOU SERIOUS?

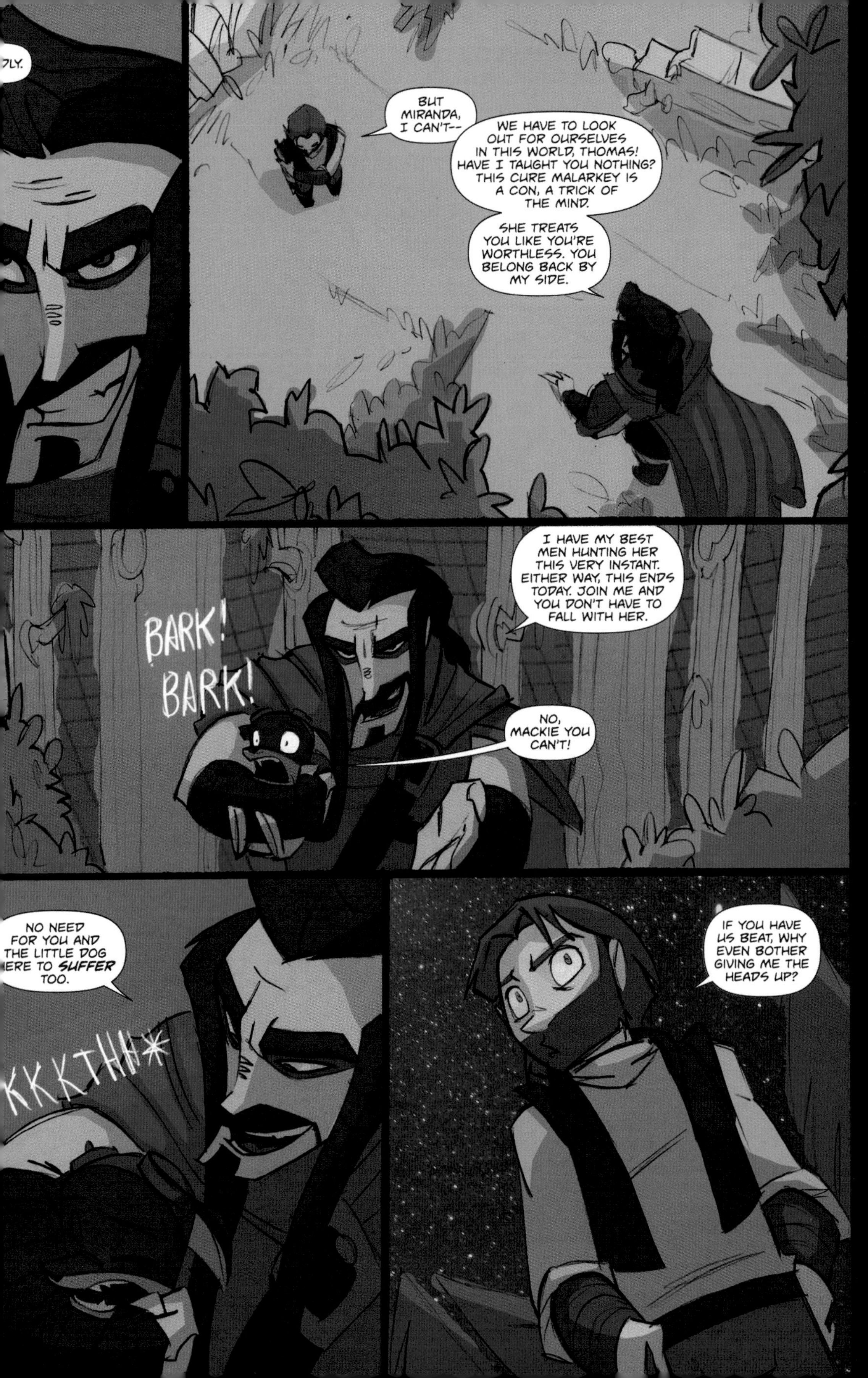

DLY.
BUT MIRANDA, I CAN'T--
WE HAVE TO LOOK OUT FOR OURSELVES IN THIS WORLD, THOMAS! HAVE I TAUGHT YOU NOTHING? THIS CURE MALARKEY IS A CON, A TRICK OF THE MIND.
SHE TREATS YOU LIKE YOU'RE WORTHLESS. YOU BELONG BACK BY MY SIDE.
I HAVE MY BEST MEN HUNTING HER THIS VERY INSTANT. EITHER WAY, THIS ENDS TODAY. JOIN ME AND YOU DON'T HAVE TO FALL WITH HER.
BARK! BARK!
NO, MACKIE YOU CAN'T!
NO NEED FOR YOU AND THE LITTLE DOG HERE TO SUFFER TOO.
KKKTHH*
IF YOU HAVE US BEAT, WHY EVEN BOTHER GIVING ME THE HEADS UP?

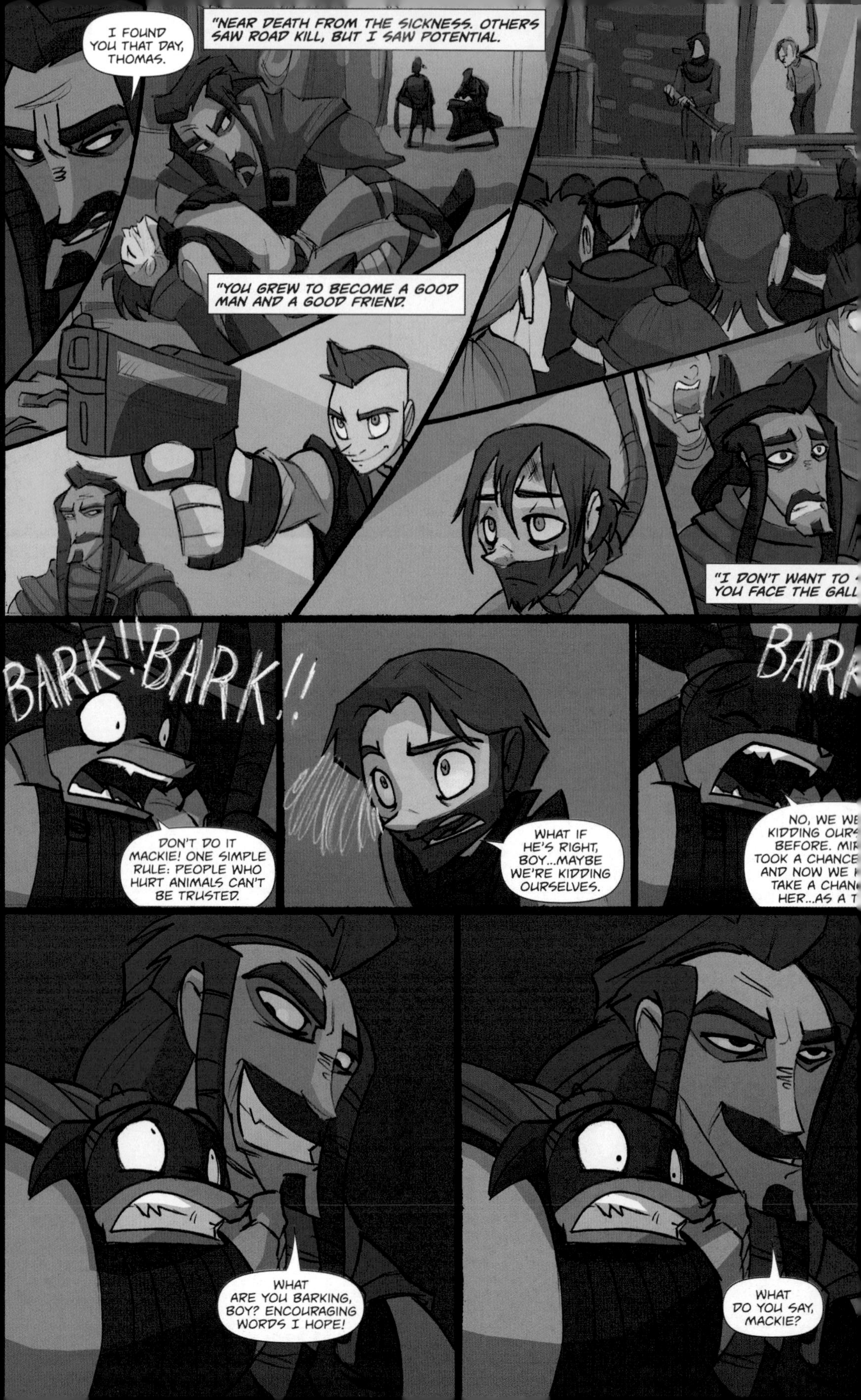
I FOUND YOU THAT DAY, THOMAS.
"NEAR DEATH FROM THE SICKNESS. OTHERS SAW ROAD KILL, BUT I SAW POTENTIAL.
"YOU GREW TO BECOME A GOOD MAN AND A GOOD FRIEND.
"I DON'T WANT TO
YOU FACE THE GALL
BARK!! BARK!!
DON'T DO IT MACKIE! ONE SIMPLE RULE: PEOPLE WHO HURT ANIMALS CAN'T BE TRUSTED.
WHAT IF HE'S RIGHT, BOY...MAYBE WE'RE KIDDING OURSELVES.
BAR
NO, WE WE
KIDDING OURS
BEFORE. MI
TOOK A CHANCE
AND NOW WE
TAKE A CHAN
HER...AS A
WHAT ARE YOU BARKING, BOY? ENCOURAGING WORDS I HOPE!
WHAT DO YOU SAY, MACKIE?

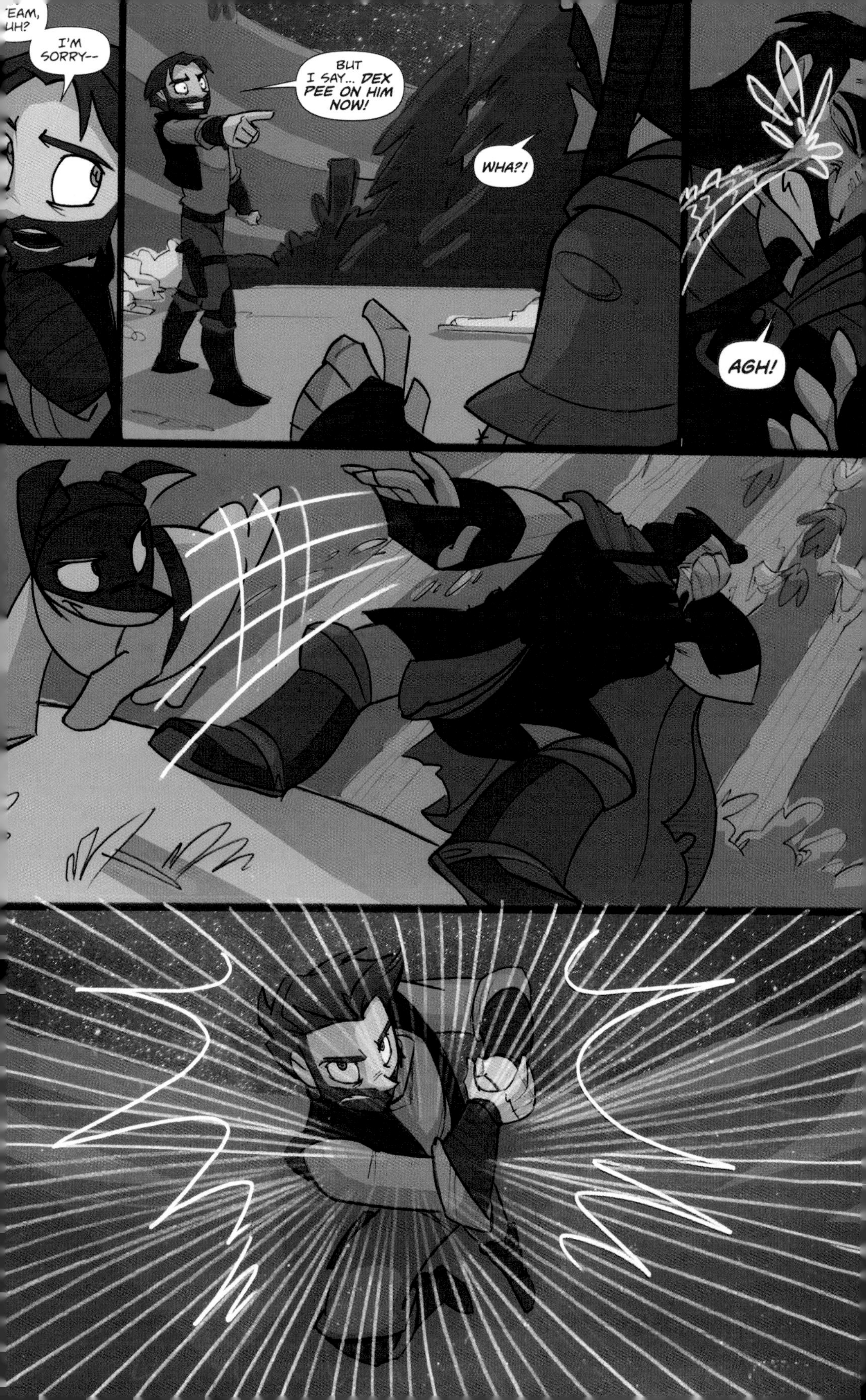
'EAM, UH?
I'M SORRY--
BUT I SAY... DEX PEE ON HIM NOW!
WHA?!
AGH!

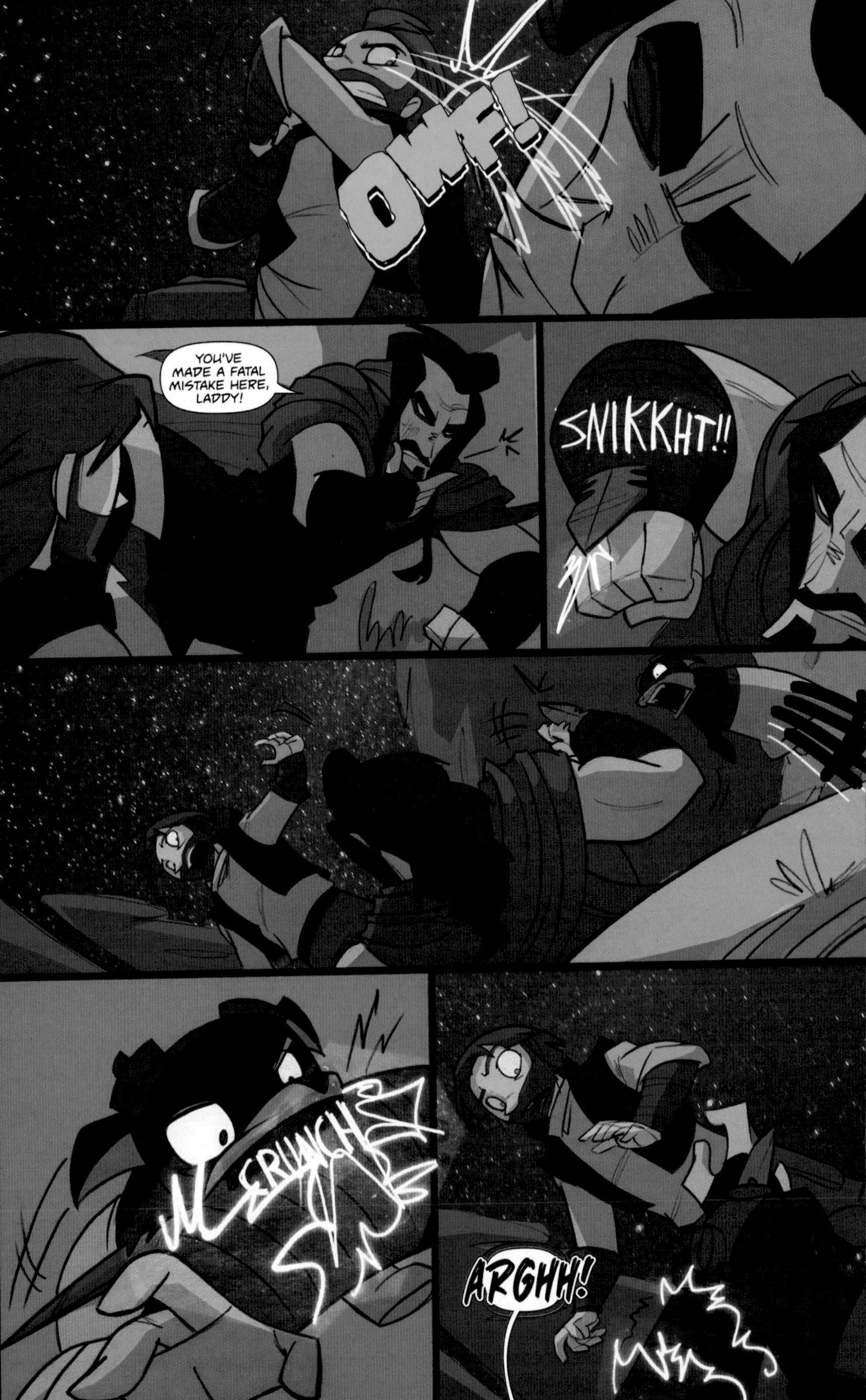
OWF!
YOU'VE MADE A FATAL MISTAKE HERE, LADDY!
SNIKKHT!!
CRUNCH
ARGHH!

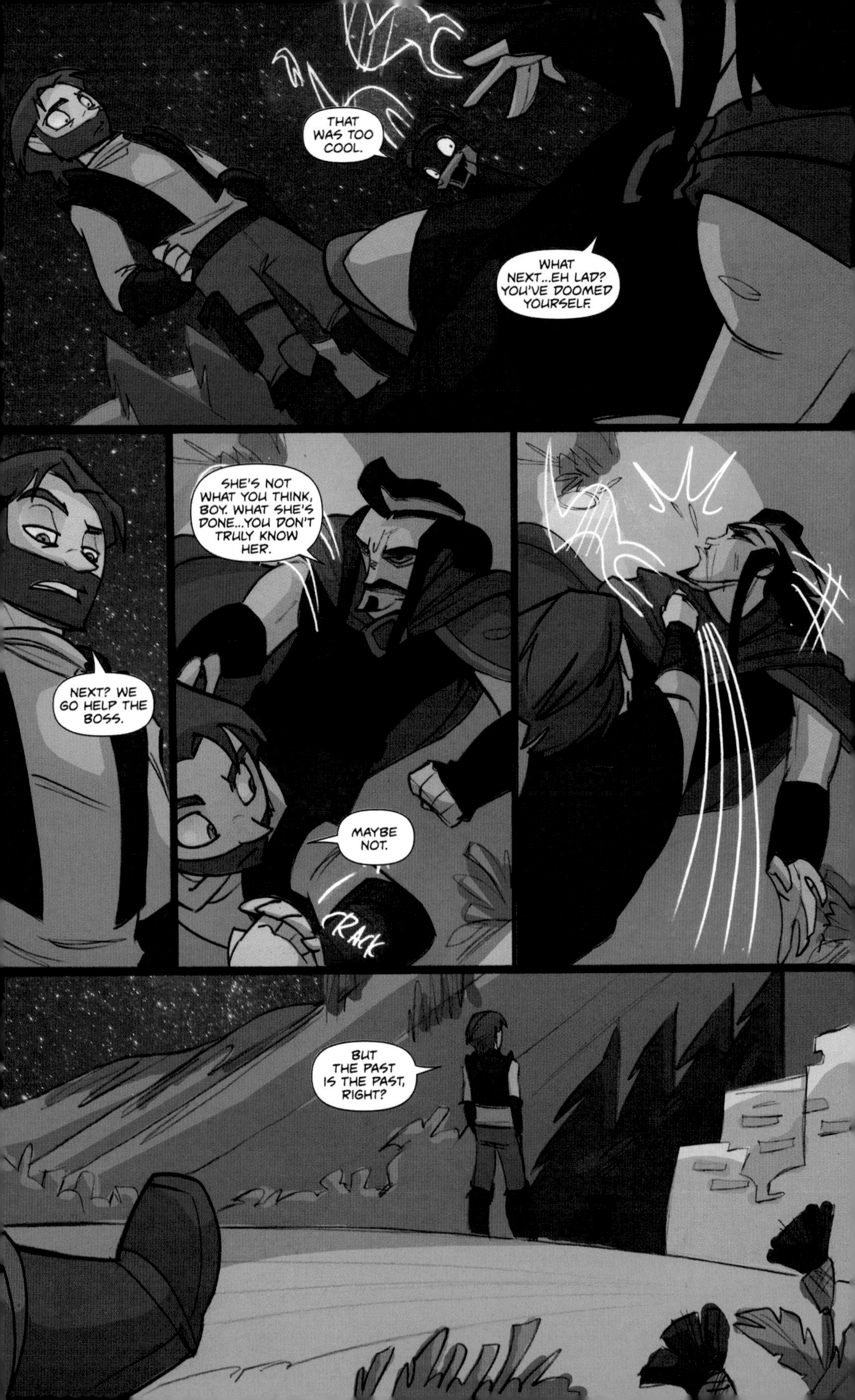
THAT WAS TOO COOL.
WHAT NEXT...EH LAD? YOU'VE DOOMED YOURSELF.
NEXT? WE GO HELP THE BOSS.
SHE'S NOT WHAT YOU THINK, BOY. WHAT SHE'S DONE...YOU DON'T TRULY KNOW HER.
MAYBE NOT.
CRACK
BUT THE PAST IS THE PAST, RIGHT?

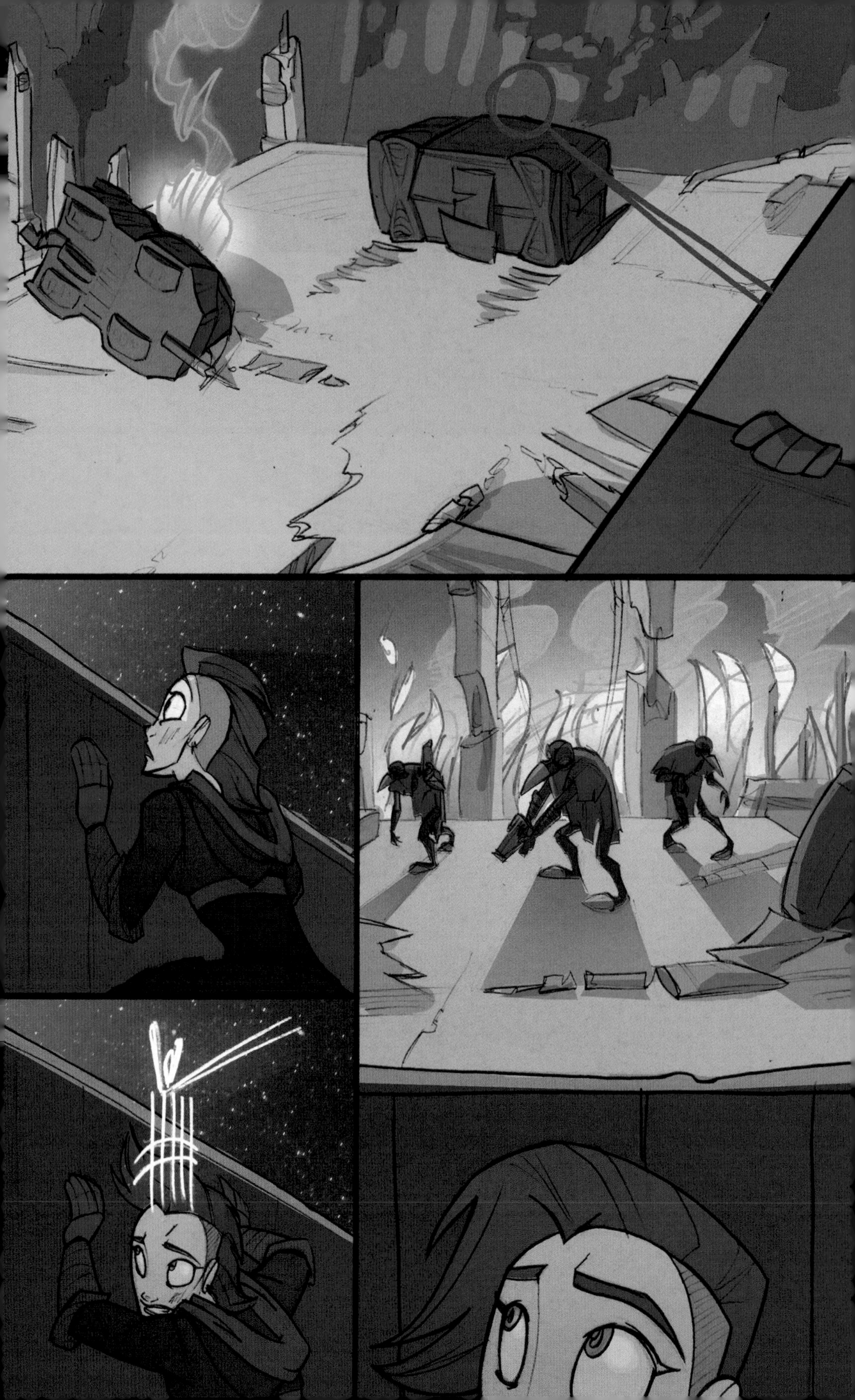

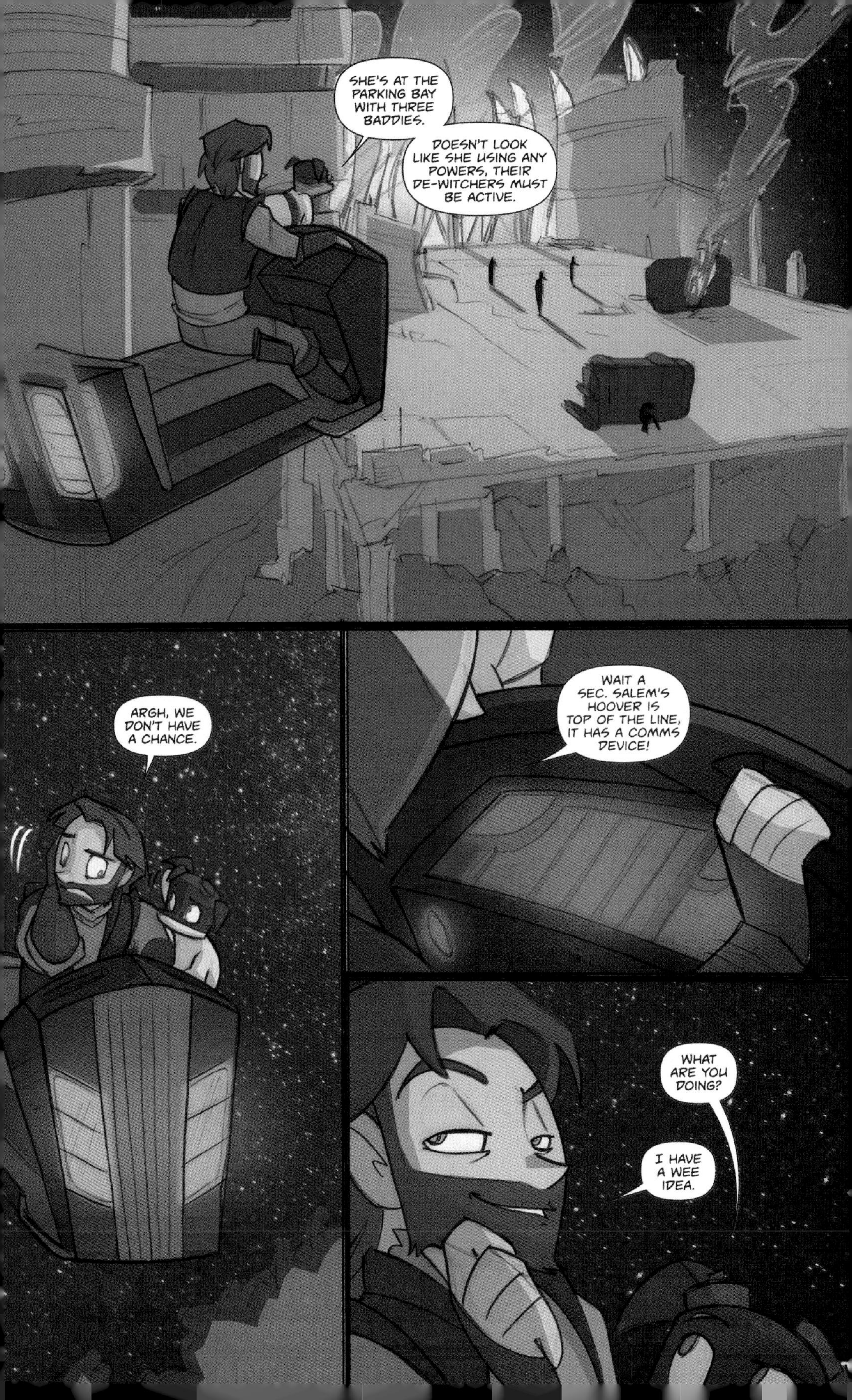
SHE'S AT THE PARKING BAY WITH THREE BADDIES.
DOESN'T LOOK LIKE SHE USING ANY POWERS, THEIR DE-WITCHERS MUST BE ACTIVE.
ARGH, WE DON'T HAVE A CHANCE.
WAIT A SEC. SALEM'S HOOVER IS TOP OF THE LINE, IT HAS A COMMS DEVICE!
WHAT ARE YOU DOING?
I HAVE A WEE IDEA.

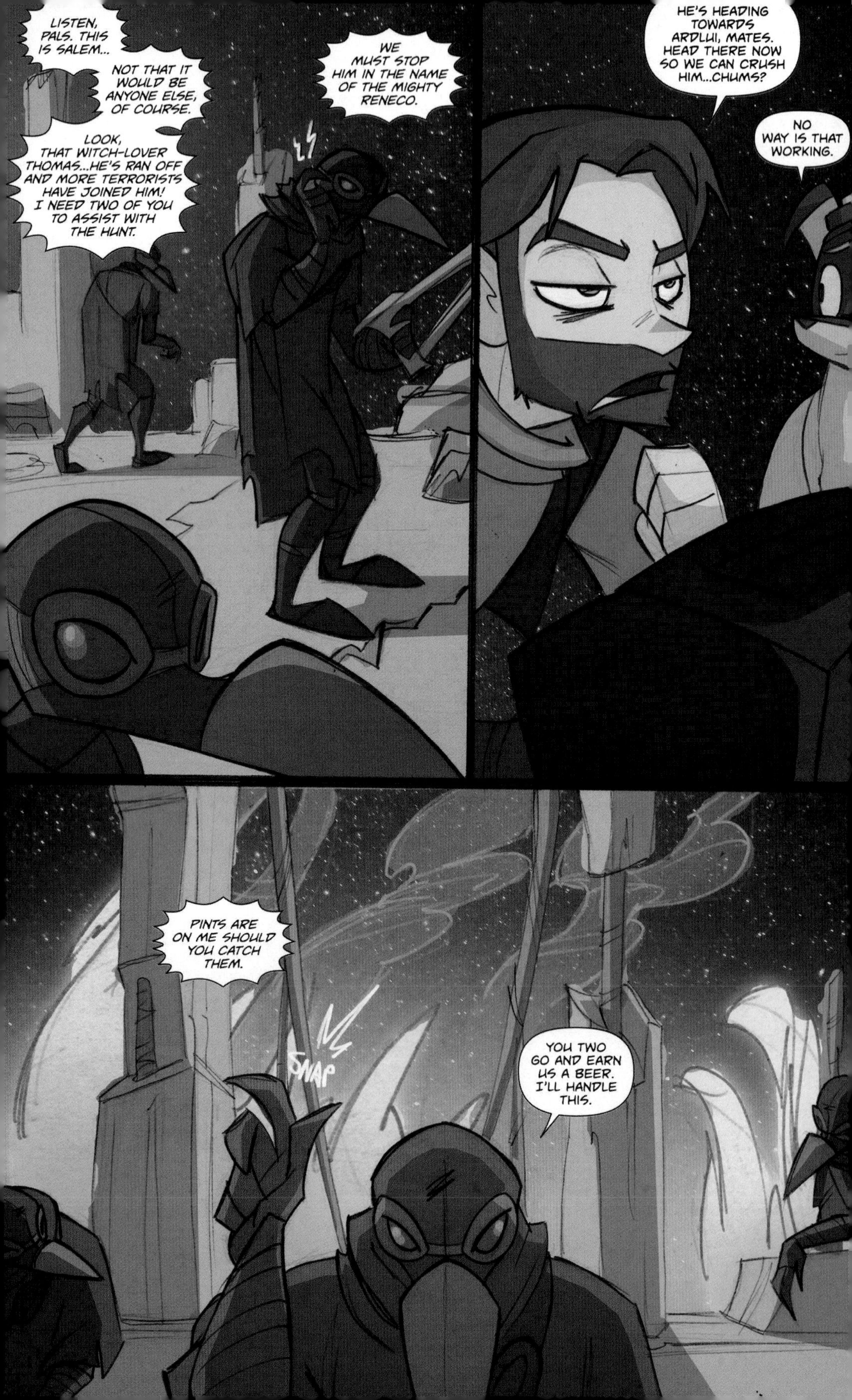
LISTEN, PALS. THIS IS SALEM...
NOT THAT IT WOULD BE ANYONE ELSE, OF COURSE.
LOOK, THAT WITCH-LOVER THOMAS...HE'S RAN OFF AND MORE TERRORISTS HAVE JOINED HIM! I NEED TWO OF YOU TO ASSIST WITH THE HUNT.
WE MUST STOP HIM IN THE NAME OF THE MIGHTY RENECO.
HE'S HEADING TOWARDS ARDLUI, MATES. HEAD THERE NOW SO WE CAN CRUSH HIM...CHUMS?
NO WAY IS THAT WORKING.
PINTS ARE ON ME SHOULD YOU CATCH THEM.
SNAP
YOU TWO GO AND EARN US A BEER. I'LL HANDLE THIS.

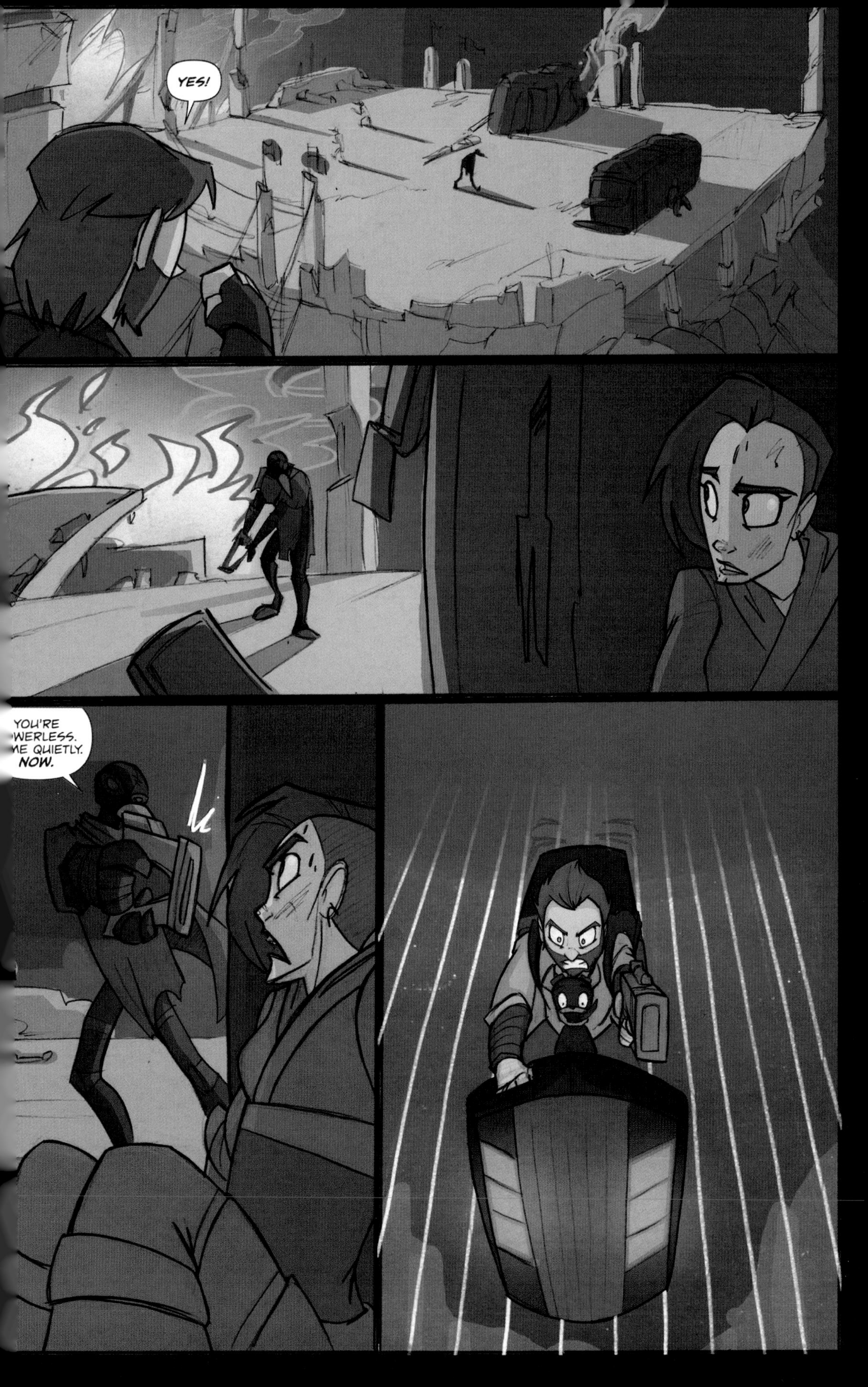
YES!
YOU'RE WERLESS. ME QUIETLY. NOW.

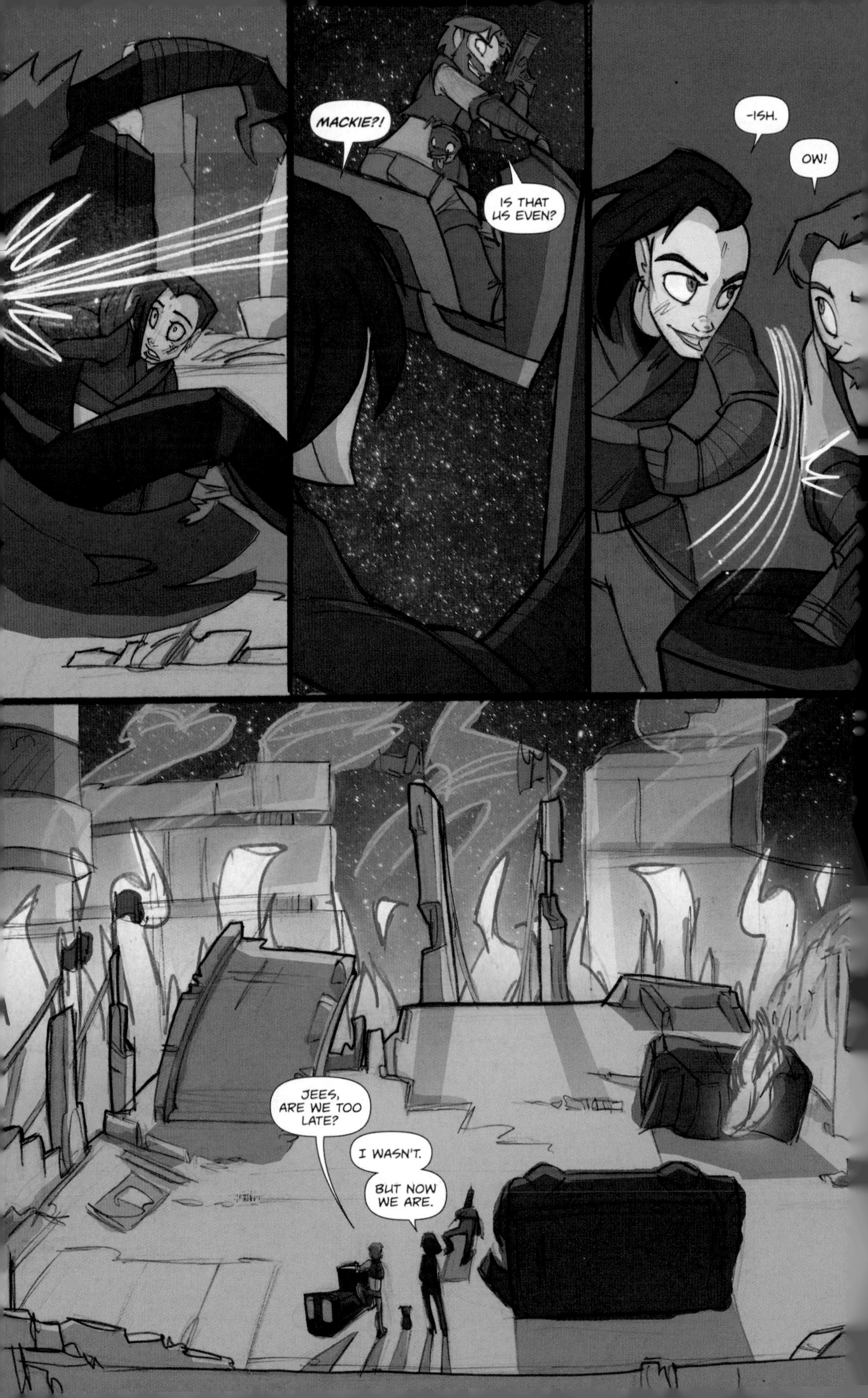
MACKIE?!
IS THAT US EVEN?
-ISH.
OW!
JEES, ARE WE TOO LATE?
I WASN'T.
BUT NOW WE ARE.

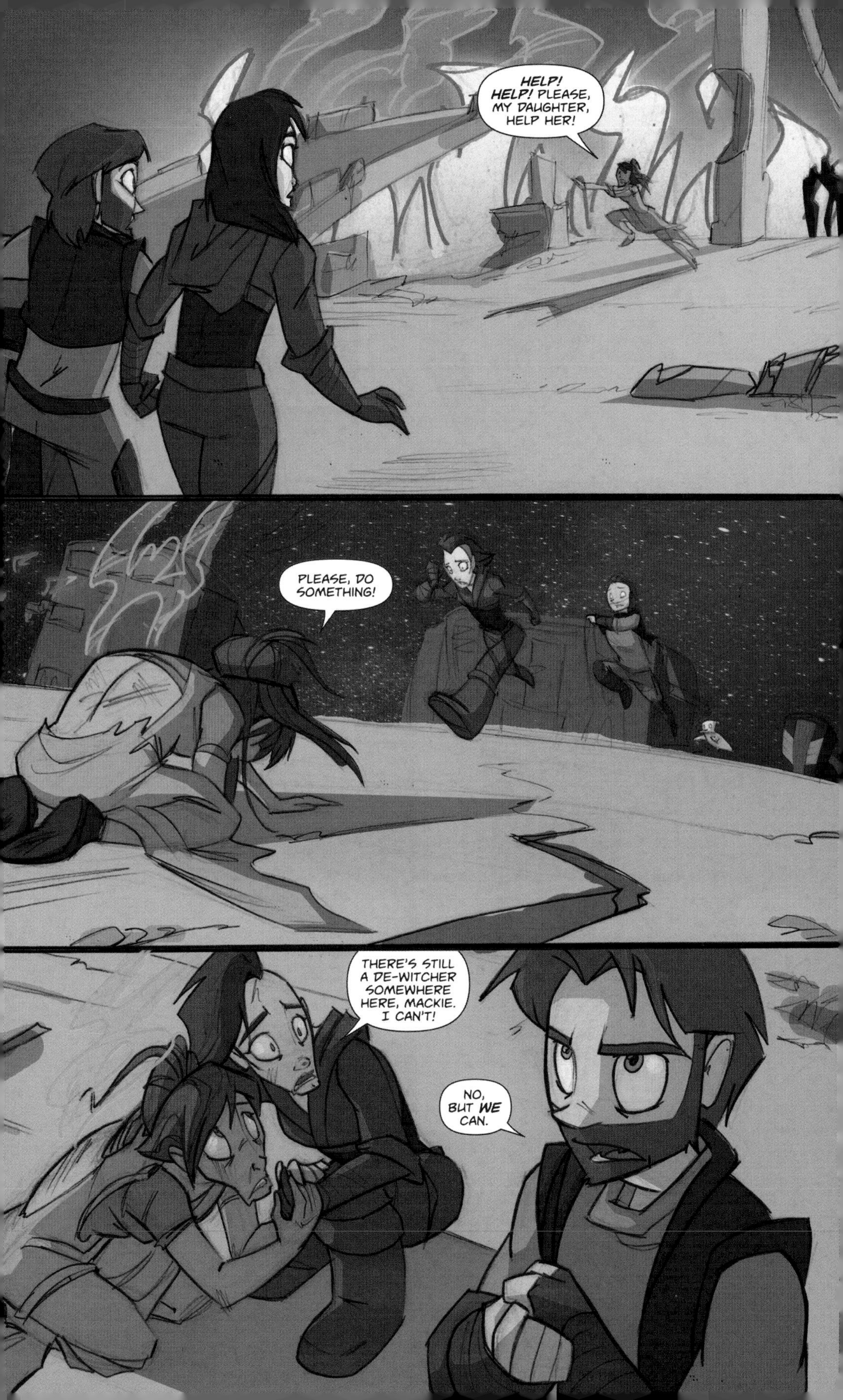
HELP! HELP! PLEASE, MY DAUGHTER, HELP HER!
PLEASE, DO SOMETHING!
THERE'S STILL A DE-WITCHER SOMEWHERE HERE, MACKIE. I CAN'T!
NO, BUT WE CAN.

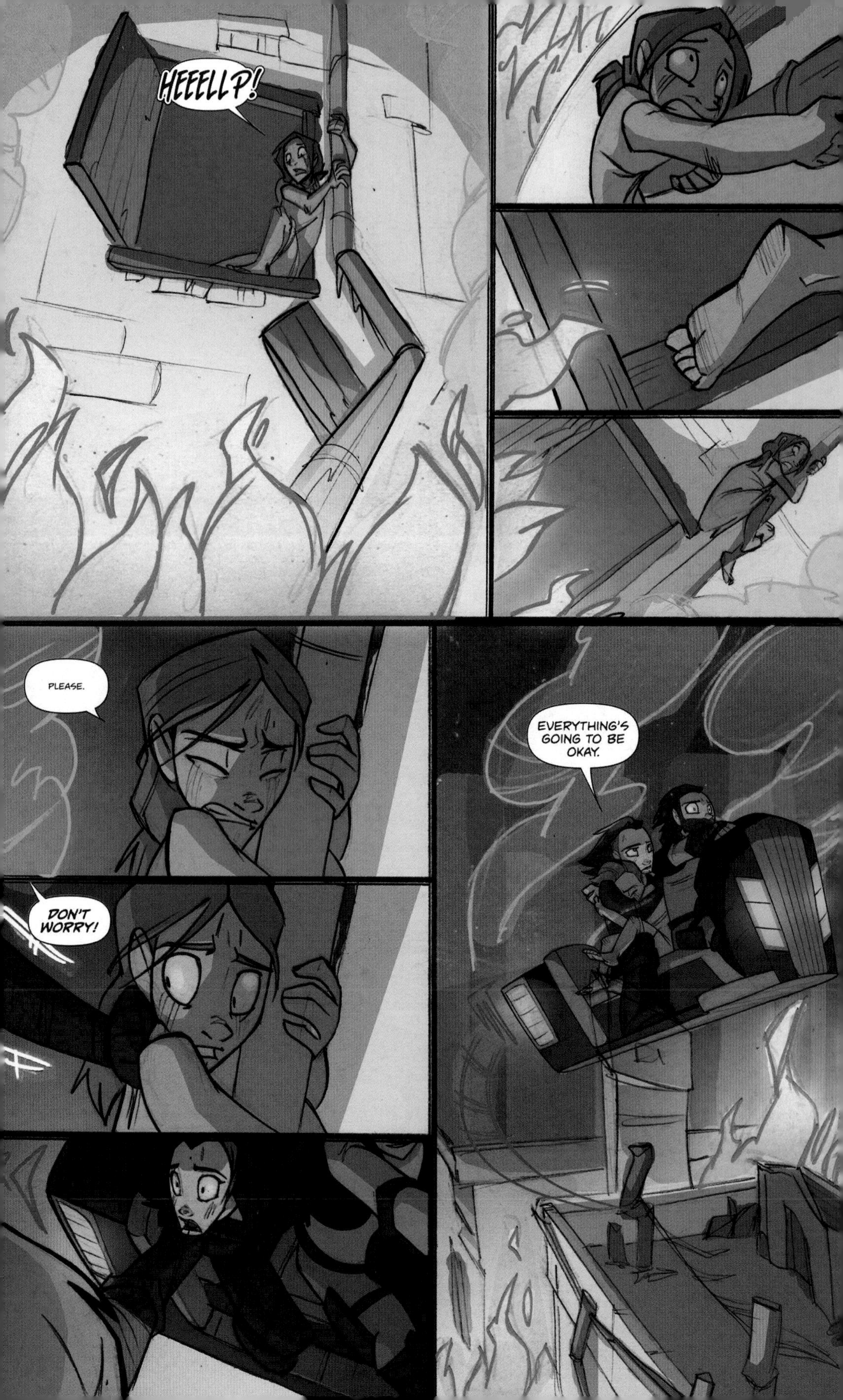
HEEELLP!
PLEASE.
DON'T WORRY!
EVERYTHING'S GOING TO BE OKAY.

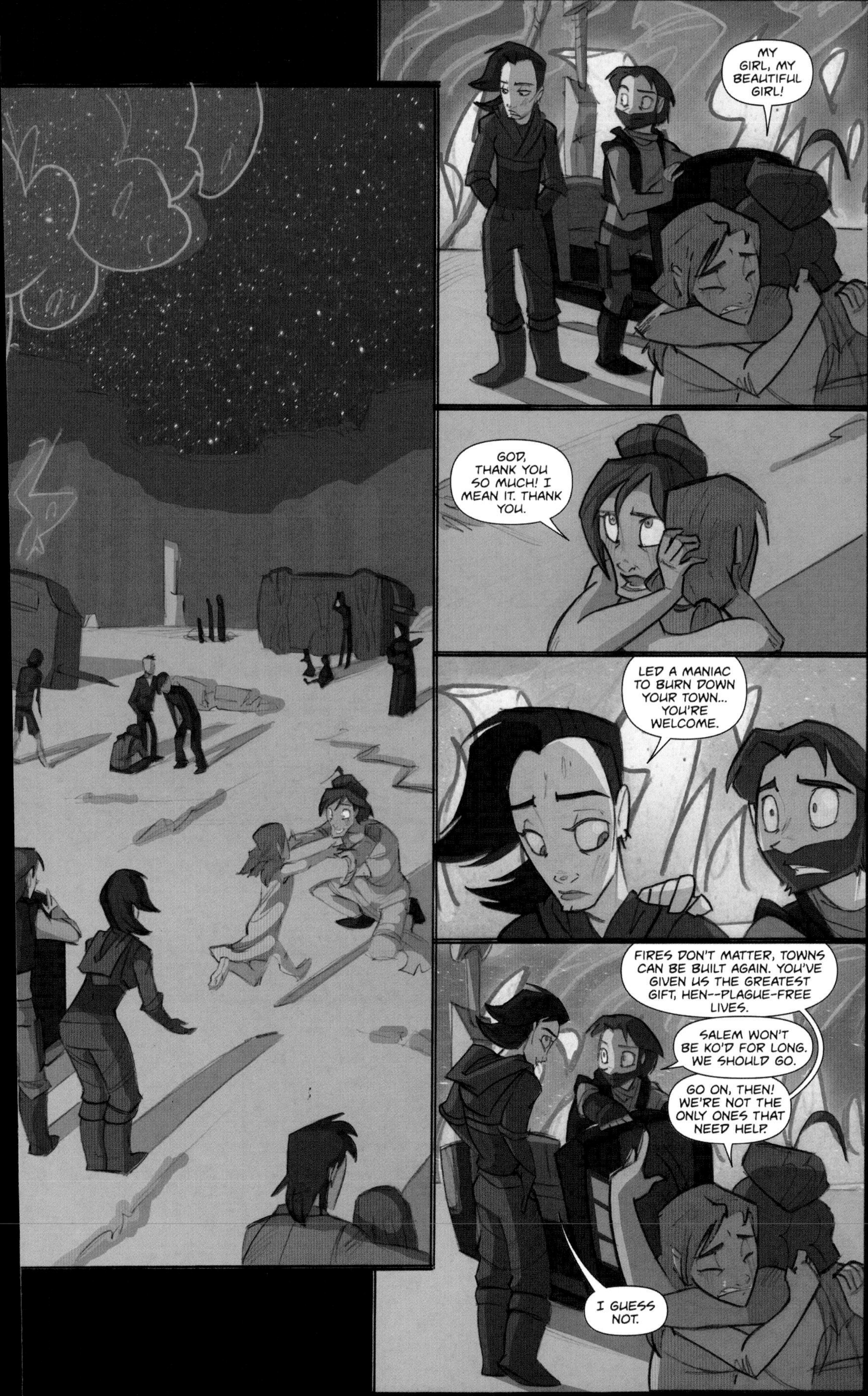
MY GIRL, MY BEAUTIFUL GIRL!
GOD, THANK YOU SO MUCH! I MEAN IT. THANK YOU.
LED A MANIAC TO BURN DOWN YOUR TOWN... YOU'RE WELCOME.
FIRES DON'T MATTER, TOWNS CAN BE BUILT AGAIN. YOU'VE GIVEN US THE GREATEST GIFT, HEN--PLAGUE-FREE LIVES.
SALEM WON'T BE KO'D FOR LONG. WE SHOULD GO.
GO ON, THEN! WE'RE NOT THE ONLY ONES THAT NEED HELP.
I GUESS NOT.

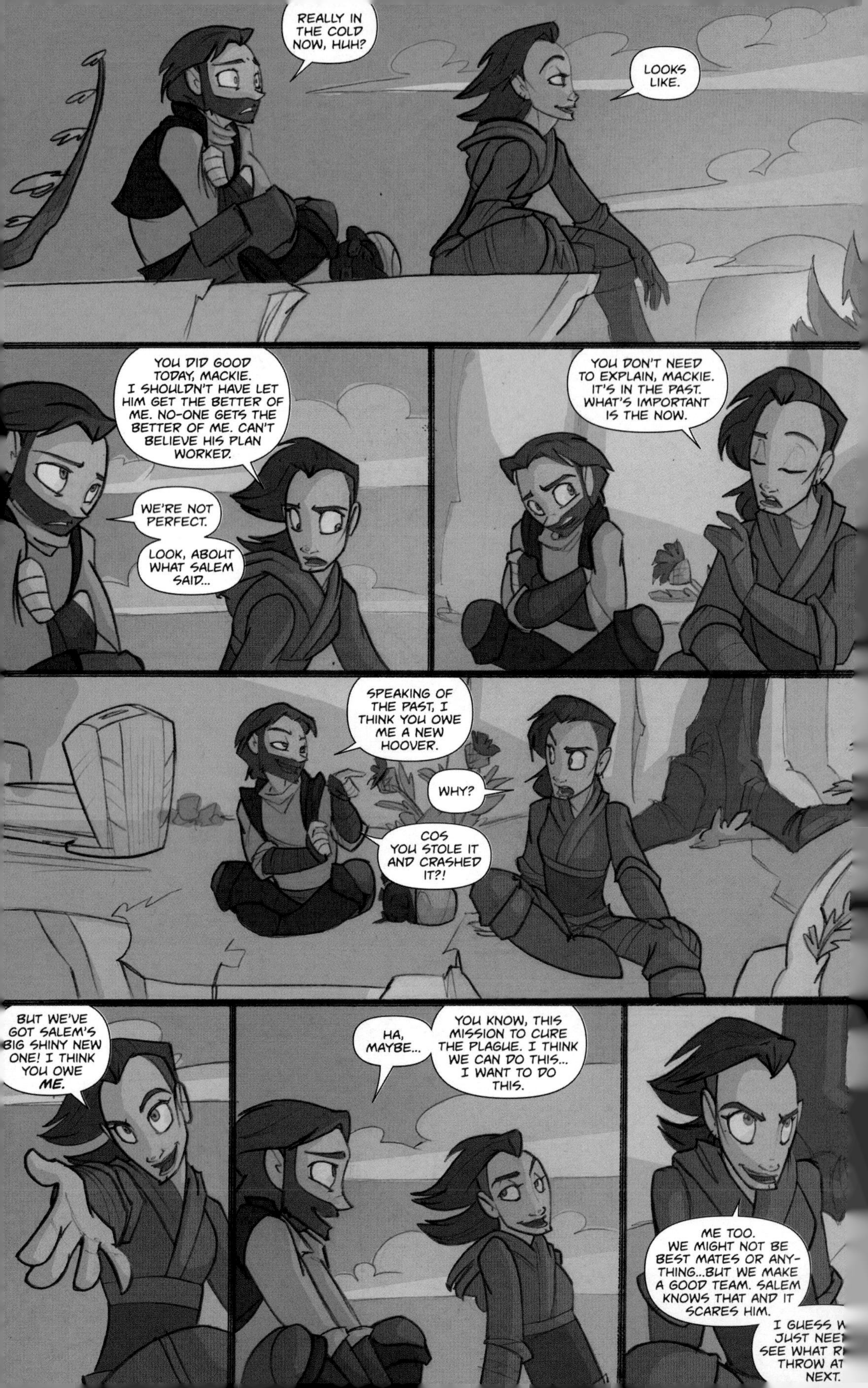
REALLY IN THE COLD NOW, HUH?
LOOKS LIKE.
YOU DID GOOD TODAY, MACKIE. I SHOULDN'T HAVE LET HIM GET THE BETTER OF ME. NO-ONE GETS THE BETTER OF ME. CAN'T BELIEVE HIS PLAN WORKED.
WE'RE NOT PERFECT.
LOOK, ABOUT WHAT SALEM SAID...
YOU DON'T NEED TO EXPLAIN, MACKIE. IT'S IN THE PAST. WHAT'S IMPORTANT IS THE NOW.
SPEAKING OF THE PAST, I THINK YOU OWE ME A NEW HOOVER.
WHY?
COS YOU STOLE IT AND CRASHED IT?!
BUT WE'VE GOT SALEM'S BIG SHINY NEW ONE! I THINK YOU OWE **ME.**
HA, MAYBE...
YOU KNOW, THIS MISSION TO CURE THE PLAGUE. I THINK WE CAN DO THIS... I WANT TO DO THIS.
ME TOO. WE MIGHT NOT BE BEST MATES OR ANY-THING...BUT WE MAKE A GOOD TEAM. SALEM KNOWS THAT AND IT SCARES HIM.

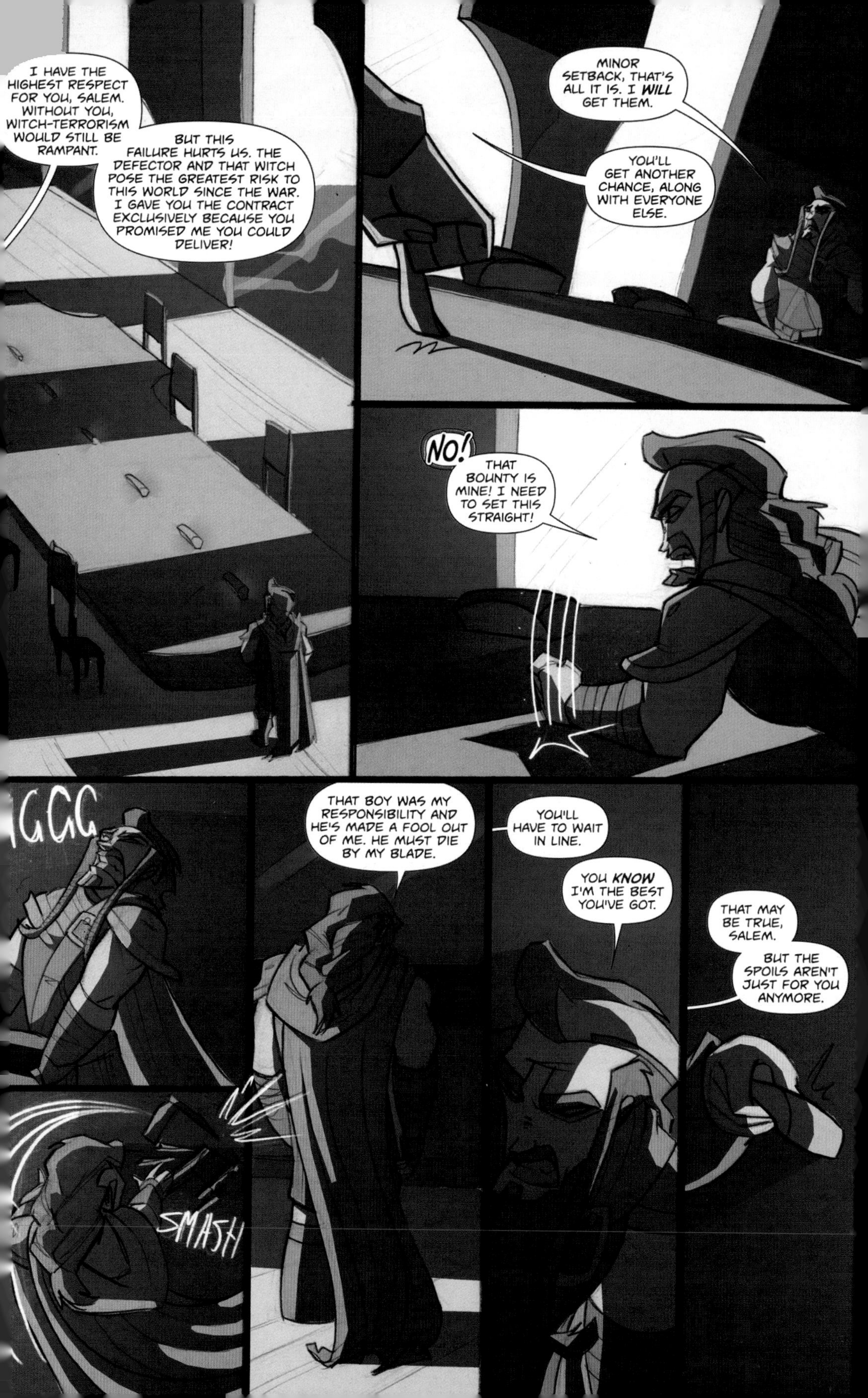
I HAVE THE HIGHEST RESPECT FOR YOU, SALEM. WITHOUT YOU, WITCH-TERRORISM WOULD STILL BE RAMPANT.
BUT THIS FAILURE HURTS US. THE DEFECTOR AND THAT WITCH POSE THE GREATEST RISK TO THIS WORLD SINCE THE WAR. I GAVE YOU THE CONTRACT EXCLUSIVELY BECAUSE YOU PROMISED ME YOU COULD DELIVER!
MINOR SETBACK, THAT'S ALL IT IS. I *WILL* GET THEM.
YOU'LL GET ANOTHER CHANCE, ALONG WITH EVERYONE ELSE.
NO!
THAT BOUNTY IS MINE! I NEED TO SET THIS STRAIGHT!
GGG
SMASH
THAT BOY WAS MY RESPONSIBILITY AND HE'S MADE A FOOL OUT OF ME. HE MUST DIE BY MY BLADE.
YOU'LL HAVE TO WAIT IN LINE.
YOU *KNOW* I'M THE BEST YOU'VE GOT.
THAT MAY BE TRUE, SALEM.
BUT THE SPOILS AREN'T JUST FOR YOU ANYMORE.

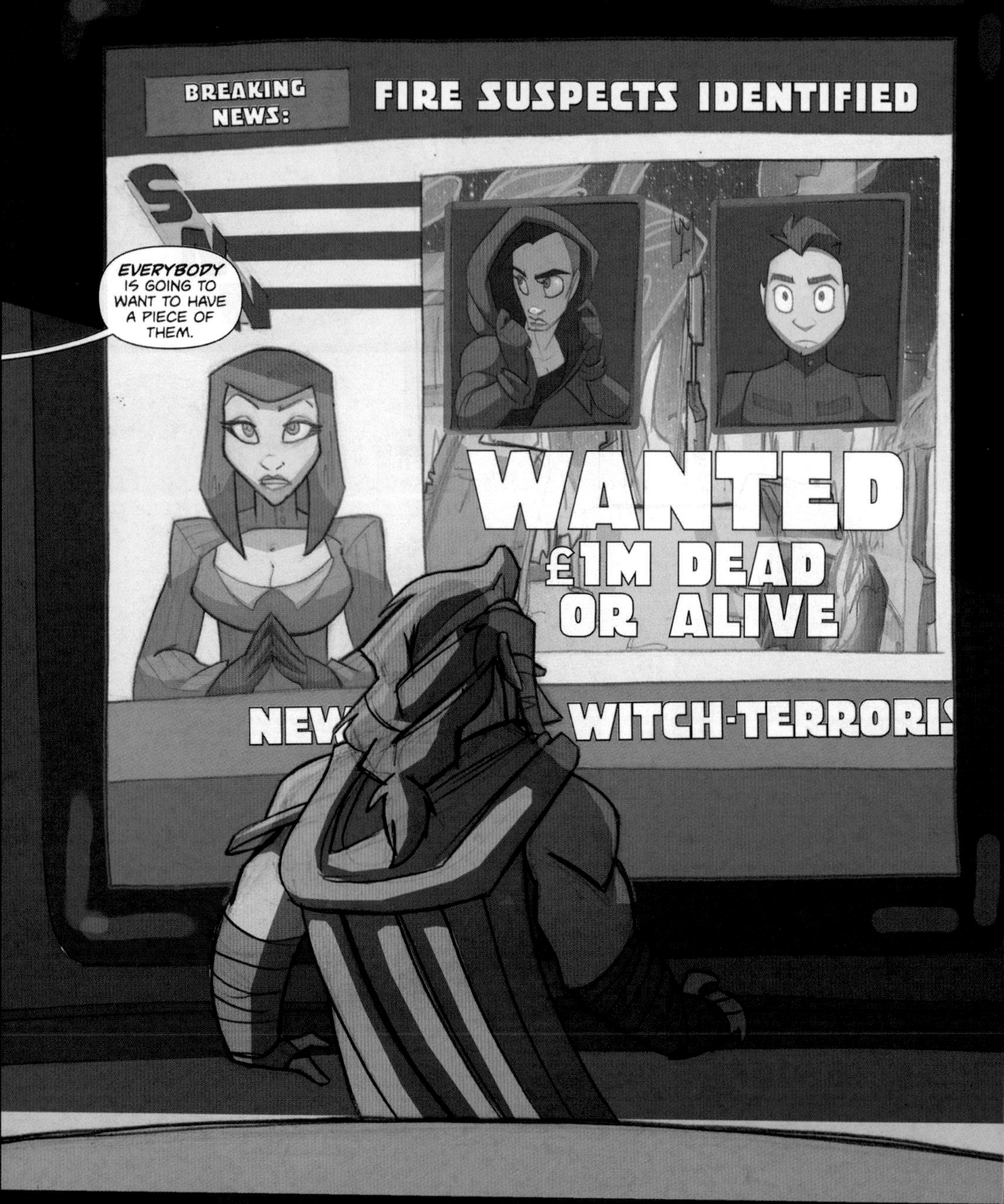

BREAKING NEWS:
FIRE SUSPECTS IDENTIFIED
EVERYBODY IS GOING TO WANT TO HAVE A PIECE OF THEM.
WANTED
£1M DEAD OR ALIVE
NEW
WITCH-TERRORIS

BONUS MATERIAL

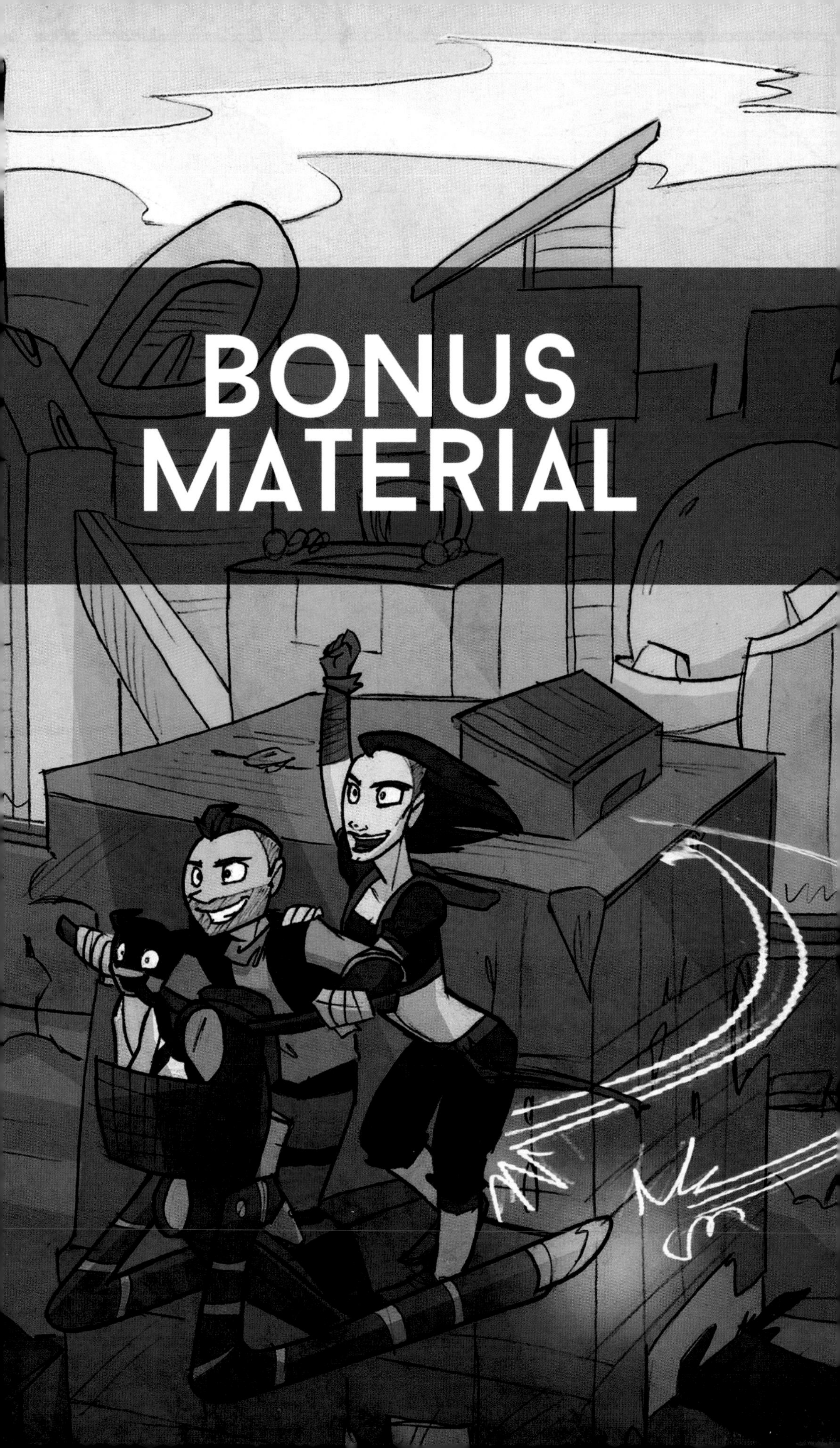

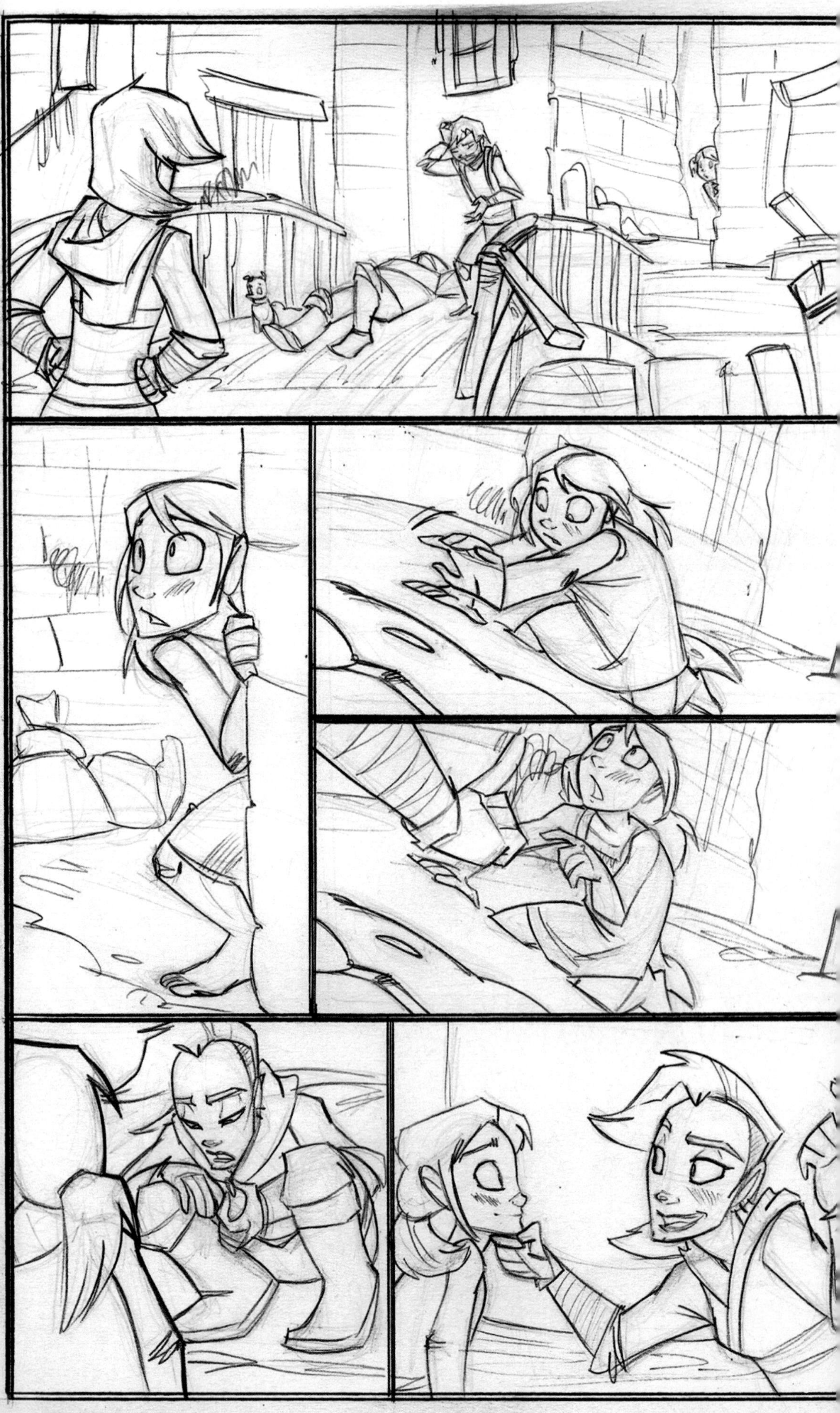

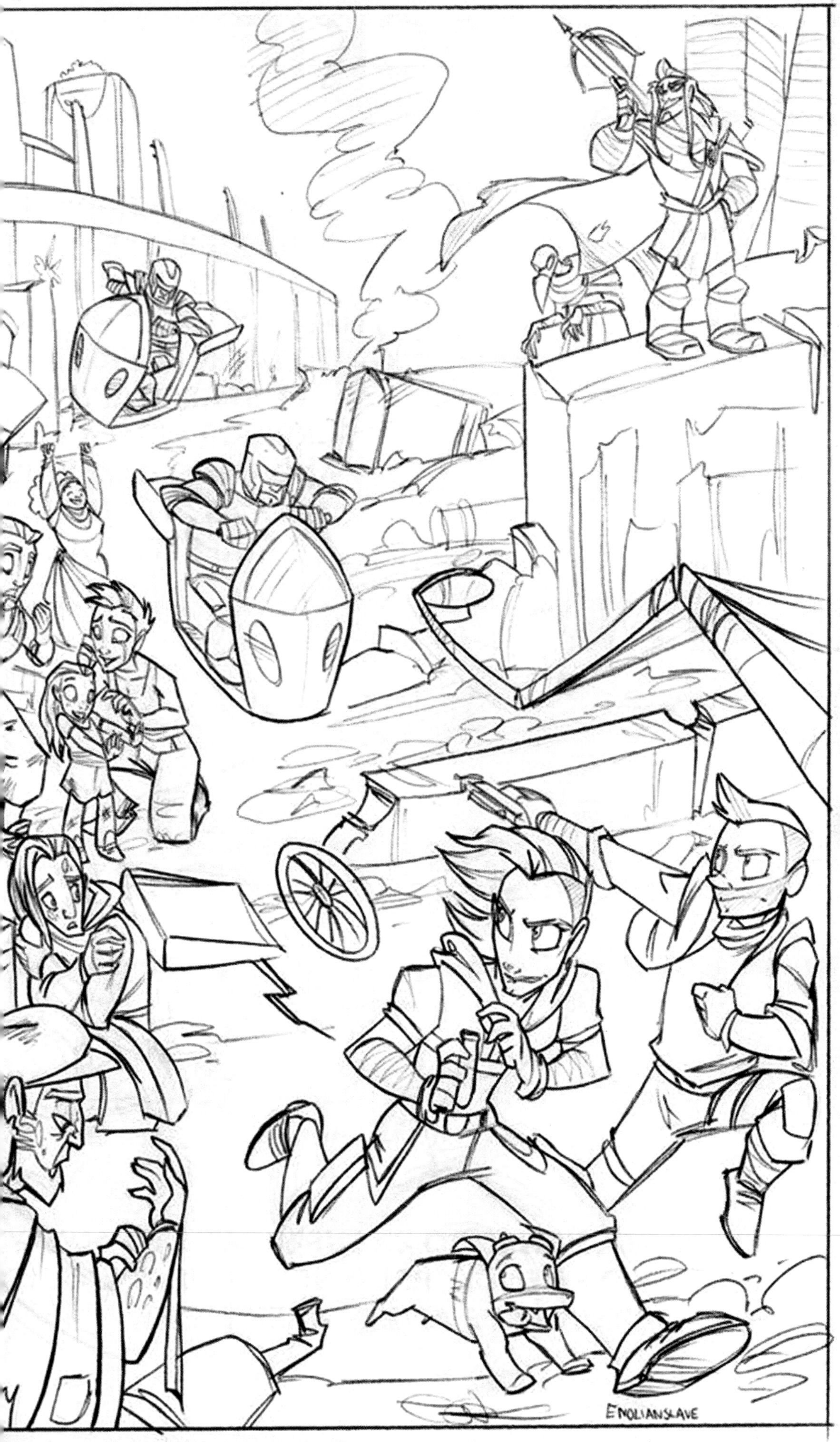
ENOLIANSLAVE

MACKIE

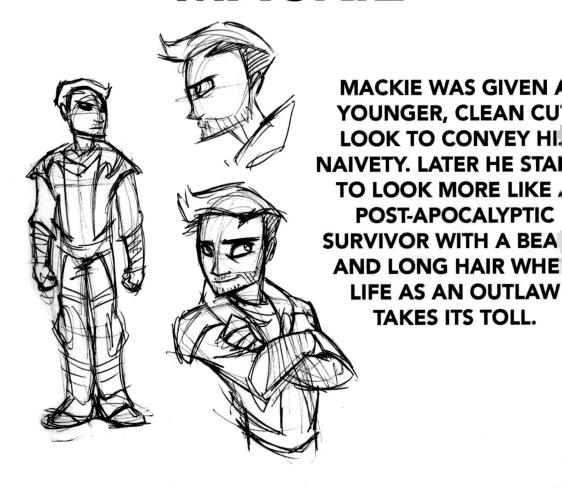

MACKIE WAS GIVEN A YOUNGER, CLEAN CUT LOOK TO CONVEY HIS NAIVETY. LATER HE STARTS TO LOOK MORE LIKE A POST-APOCALYPTIC SURVIVOR WITH A BEARD AND LONG HAIR WHEN LIFE AS AN OUTLAW TAKES ITS TOLL.

DEX

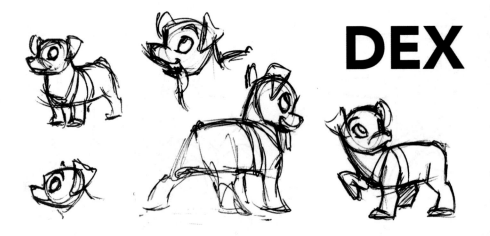

DEX WAS DESIGNED TO BE SUPER-CUTE TO ALWAYS GIVE A KID FRIENDLY PRESENCE IN WHAT WOULD USUALLY BE A VERY DARK STORY.

MIRANDA LEE

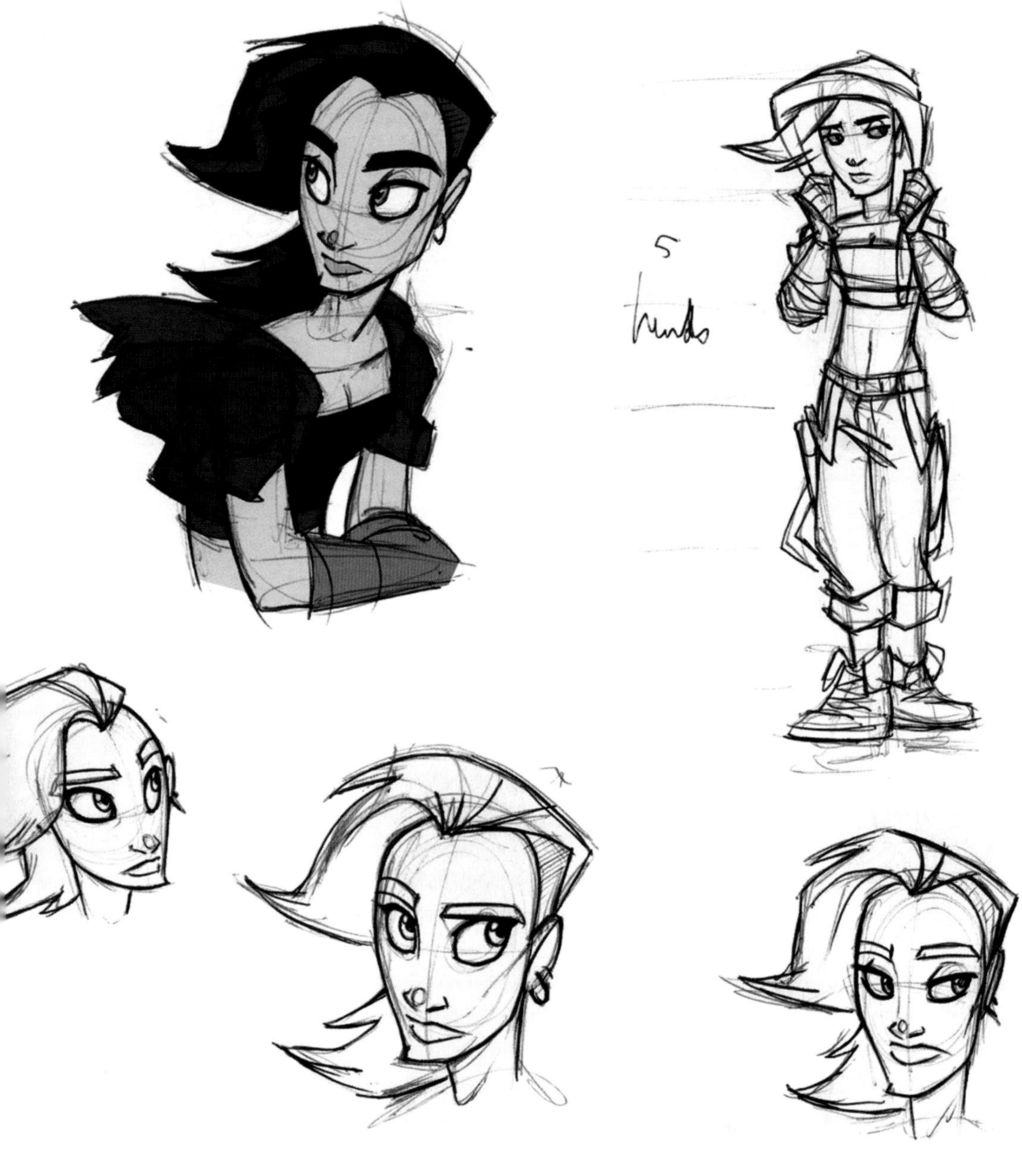

THE ONLY CHARACTER DESCRIPTION GIVEN FOR IRANDA WAS 'SHE'S PUNKY AND EARTHY'. TANYA IS AN EXPERT IN CHARACTER DESIGN SO OFTEN LESS SCRIPTION ALLOWS HER MAXIMUM CONTROL TO USE HAT TALENT. NOTICE THE SUBTLE WITCHY WART ON THE END OF HER NOSE AND THE EARTH COLOUR SCHEME OF GREEN AND BROWN.

SALEM

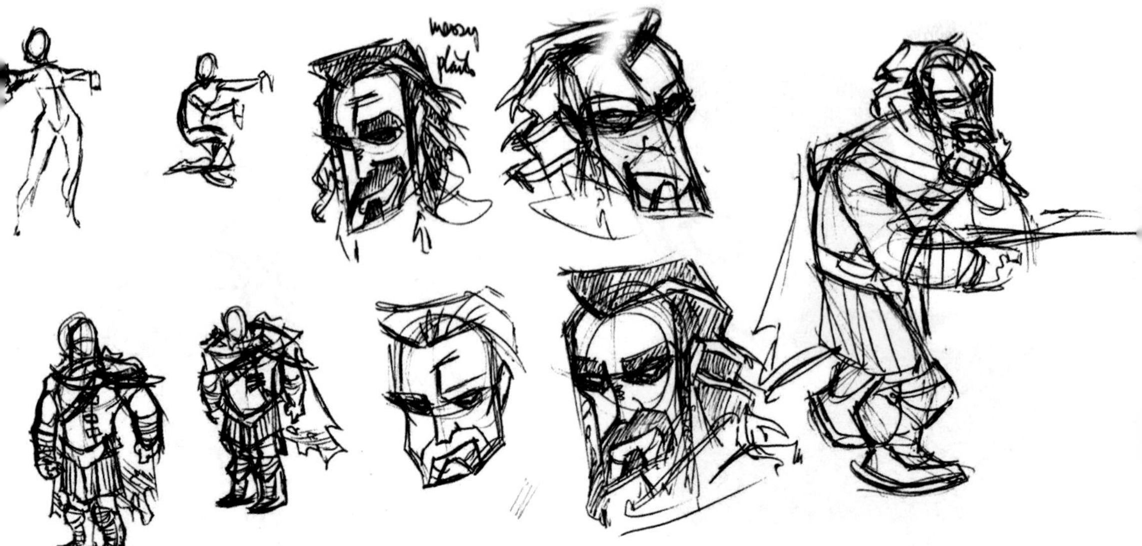

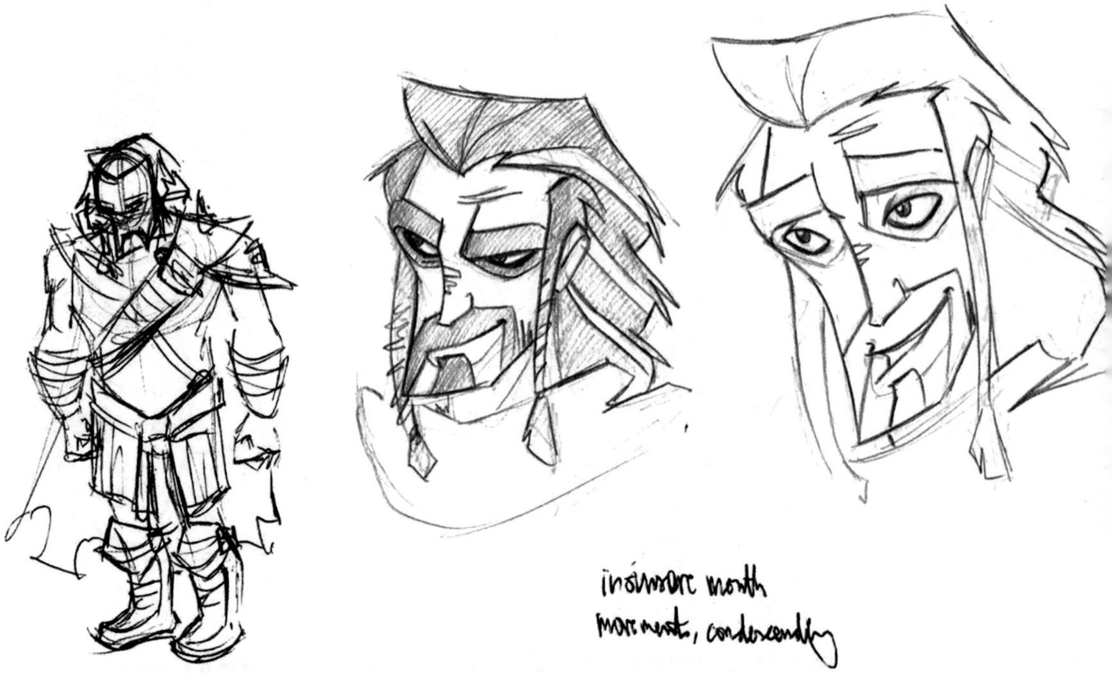

SALEM IS ONE OF OUR FAVOURITE CHARACTERS, MOSTLY DOWN TO THE VERY UNIQUE CHARACTER DESIGN. HE HAS THE FLAIR OF OLD SCOTTISH WARRIC WHO HAS YEARS OF EXPERIENCE IN BATTLE.

THE HOOVER

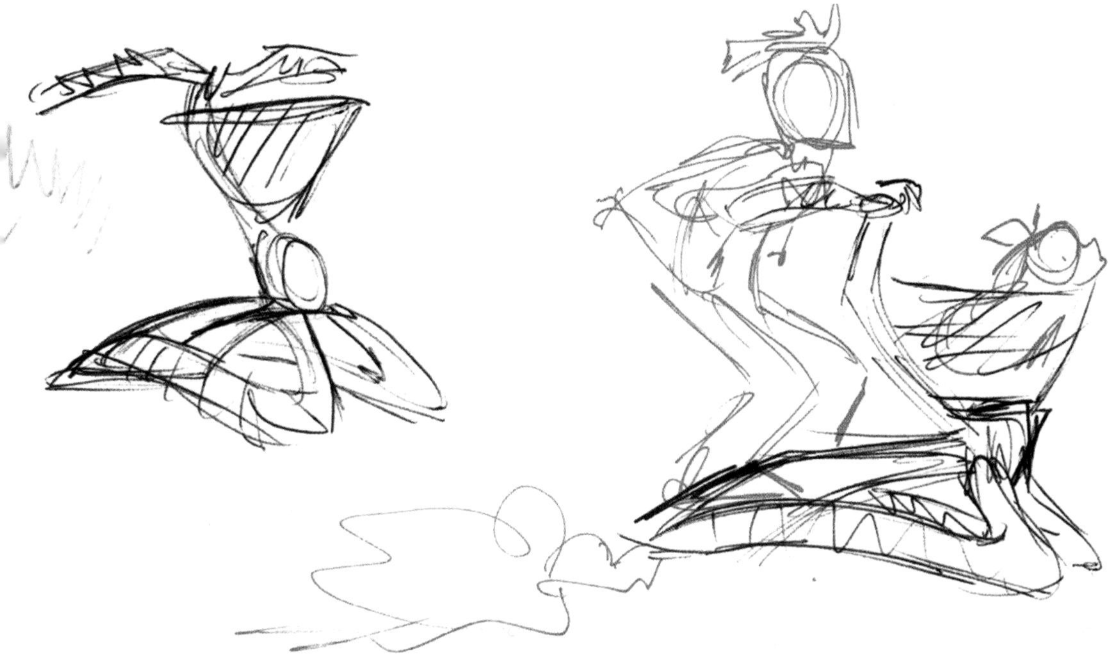

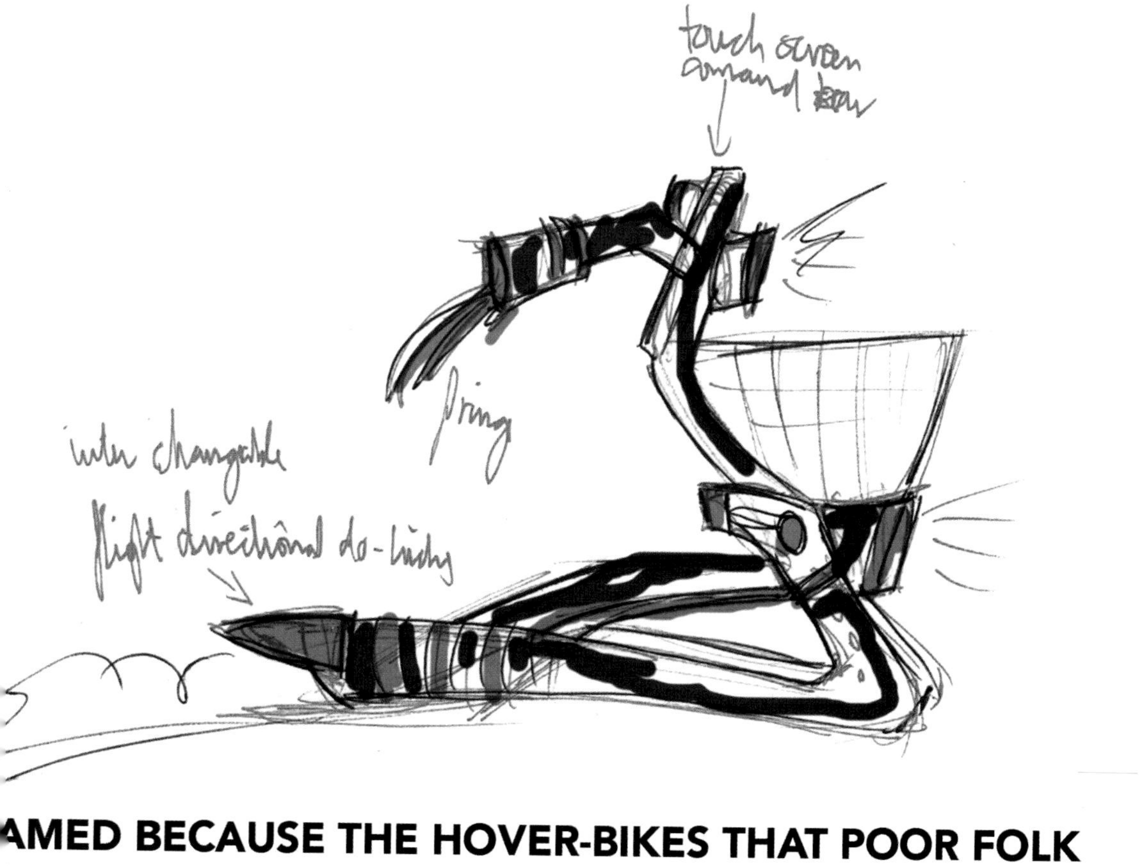
touch screen comand bar
inter changable
flight directional do-hicky

AMED BECAUSE THE HOVER-BIKES THAT POOR FOLK E ARE OFTEN CHEAP QUALITY AND SECOND HAND - AND THEREFORE SUCK.

PlAGUED ISSUE 3 EXTRACT FOR TPB VOL 1

PAGE SIXTEEN

(6 PANELS)

1 - We're now on the young girl from the beginning of the issue 2. She is crying, climbing up the side of the wall on the drain pipe, dying to escape the blaze.

GIRL: HEEELPP!

2 - She clambers on to a higher part at the side of the tall building, clutching on to the edge of the roof, trying to pull herself up.

3 - The fire rises, it's nearly reaching her feet.

4 - She closes her eyes, crying.

GIRL: PLEASE.

5 - Her eyes pop open with surprise. Miranda's hand is clutched at the back of her top.

Miranda (tail off panel above): DON'T WORRY!

6 - They fly away from the building that is now fully engulfed in flames. The girl is cradled in Miranda's arms. Miranda doesn't have the same sly confident smile she had when she first said that line previously. A sort of empty disbelief has washed over her.

MIRANDA: EVERYTHING'S GOING TO BE OKAY.

PAGE SEVENTEEN

(8 PANELS)

1 - Mackie, Miranda and Rex are all by the girl's mother at the carpark. The Hoover is parked and Miranda is letting the girl out of her arms.

2 - The girl runs over to her mum's open arms.

MUM: MY GIRL, MY BEAUTIFUL GIRL!

3 - The girl hugs into her, the mother looks onwards to Mackie and Miranda, gratefully.

MOTHER: GOD, THANK YOU SO MUCH! I MEAN IT. THANK YOU.

4 - Miranda now glumly looks the other way, leaning against the hoover. The mother gets emotional.

MIRANDA: LED A MANIAC TO BURN DOWN YOUR TOWN… YOU'RE WELCOME.

MOTHER: FIRES DON'T MATTER, TOWNS CAN BE BUILT AGAIN. YOU'VE GIVEN US THE GREATEST GIFT, HEN -- PLAGUE-FREE LIVES.

6 - Mackie puts his hand on her shoulder. She looks upset.

MACKIE: SALEM WON'T BE KO'D FOR LONG. WE SHOULD GO.

7 - The woman shooshes her by waving her hand and tells her to go away in a motherly-way.

WOMAN: GO ON, THEN! WE'RE NOT THE ONLY ONES THAT NEED HELP.

8 - Miranda lets out a sombre smile.

MIRANDA: I GUESS NOT.

PAGE EIGHTEEN

(5 PANELS)

1 - Mackie and Miranda sit on a large rocky hill somewhere else, eating beans out of a tin. Rex is lying in-between them, sleeping. Mackie is looking up at the sky as snow begins to fall. The water bottle with the plagued cure sits next to them securely in a rucksack. (Just cause we haven't really seen it in a while).

MACKIE: REALLY IN THE COLD NOW, HUH?

MIRANDA: LOOKS LIKE.

2 - Miranda looks over to Mackie in a sincere way. Mackie looks down at his beans.

MIRANDA: YOU DID GOOD TODAY, MACKIE. I SHOULDN'T HAVE LET HIM GET THE BETTER OF ME. NO-ONE GETS THE BETTER OF ME. CAN'T BELIEVE HIS PLAN WORKED.

MACKIE: WE'RE NOT PERFECT.
LOOK, ABOUT WHAT SALEM SAID...

3 - Miranda puts her hand up and looks emotional yet sincere.

MIRANDA: YOU DON'T NEED TO EXPLAIN, MACKIE. IT'S IN THE PAST. WHAT'S IMPORTANT IS THE NOW.

4 - Mackie gives Miranda an annoyed scrunched face. Miranda looks defensive, in a light 'oopsie' kind of way.

MACKIE: SPEAKING OF THE PAST, I THINK YOU OWE ME A NEW HOOVER.

MIRANDA: WHY?

MACKIE: 'COS YOU STOLE IT AND CRASHED IT?!

MIRANDA: BUT WE'VE GOT SALEM'S BIG SHINY NEW ONE! I THINK YOU OWE ME.

5 - Mackie lets out a sort of sombre smile. Miranda smiles too.

MACKIE: HA, MAYBE...
YOU KNOW, THIS MISSION TO CURE THE PLAGUE. I THINK WE CAN DO THIS... I WANT TO DO THIS.